The Down Johns Collection:

Stories of Ugly Truths

By Traci Dolan-Priestley

This is sort of a work of fiction. The author fully intends for you to recognize, in spirit, characters, places, and incidents, perhaps even yourself, family, friends, coworkers, or acquaintances of any of the aforementioned, especially if you live or have lived or know someone who lives or has lived in Appalachia or a small town. Resemblance to actual events and locales might happen, but only if you know me personally. Some resemblances really are coincidental. Just be glad I didn't call anyone out by their real name.

Copyright @ 2016 by Traci Dolan-Priestley

ISBN 978-1-84914-946-4

CreateSpace

Cover art by Erica Lorenz Hays

Printed in the United States of America

For Gary and Nate

The Down Johns Collection:
Stories of Ugly Truths

Down Johns

The shacks sit in the bottomland beside the river. Unless you know they are there, you may drive by and, only as an afterthought, realize you saw the edge of a brown-shingled roof or the glint of sunlight on tin. They are a little more noticeable in winter when the coal dusted weeds and brambles die off.

The shack with the brown shingled roof leans to the right. The sun has baked the shack, like all the shacks in Down Johns, until the boards have shrunk and separated. Rags, yellowed newspapers, and moldy pages from the Sears & Roebuck catalog are stuffed in the gaps to keep bugs and vermin out. This homemade insulation doesn't help during the cold of winter. In summer the air is thick and stifling hot from the coal cook stove. Their unshod mattresses are marred with body-shaped sweat stains and a smell, both sweet and rank.

There are seven children who live here and two daughters who are buried on a distant plot of land that belongs to a family member. The children go barefoot during the summer, their feet calloused from walking on river rocks and the packed dirt path that runs from the shanties to the outhouse, the river, and up the hillside to the blacktop.

Their father, Arlie, is a thin, wiry man with a hacking, moist cough who most often sits on their front stoop whittling. He sells his creations by the roadside on Saturdays. One of his daughters, Doris, the third from the oldest, sits with him. She spends her time changing the ragged clothes on a homemade doll, drool pooling along her bottom lip until it overflows, sometimes running down her chin, sometimes stretching in iridescent strands to her chest. Her father puts down his knife, reaches over, and wipes her face with a limp handkerchief faded by its long afternoons on the clothesline. The doctors called her retarded, an imbecile, and had encouraged them to send her to the state hospital.

"To do what?" her father had asked. The doctor had taken a deep breath and explained more about the hospital while her mother, Louisa, sat with her lips pursed. Louisa was pregnant with their fifth child, and as they walked down the street to meet her brother - they didn't own a car - she had pressed the handkerchief into his chest, and said, "You want her, you take care of her." She had enough to worry about with three other children, one still in diapers, and one on the way. It had been her way of telling him she wanted the girl to go to the hospital, to wash her hands of Doris, her way of rebelling.

Today though, Louisa steps out of the shanty without speaking to either of them.

"Where you goin'?"

It is not as though she could go far on her bare feet in her threadbare housedress, her hair in a loose bun, tendrils clinging to her sweaty skin.

"Miss Lettie's," she says, and walks away, not even hearing him ask why.

The dirt path winds through the trees and at the outhouse it branches left onto another path. Miss Lettie's shanty sits further back in the bottom toward the road. Louisa hears the children splashing in the river. She wishes she could strip out of the damp dress and sink into the water, down, down deep to where the icy current tugs at your feet or lie down and press her burning face onto the packed, naked earth. Instead, she stays on the path to Miss Lettie's open door. Mrs. Lettie Combs is a widow, her husband succumbed to the mines suddenly, unlike Arlie with his moist, hacking cough and no Social Security because the mine owner didn't see fit to contribute, and he didn't see fit to argue, no cure for the cough, and their twelve year age difference may as well have been fifty.

As her eyes adjust, Louisa sees Miss Lettie at her quilt loom, her gnarled fingers drawing white thread from the underside to the top and down again in perfect stitches, equally spaced and equally spanning the material. Her son, who has a government job in the city, buys her material and sells the quilts for her. She makes a small living, more if her

7

son didn't skim from her. She doesn't read, write, or cipher and there's no one to tell her any different.

"Miss Louisa, what can I do for you?"

Louisa doesn't answer. She's not quite sure how to answer. She clasps her hands at her waist and clears her throat.

"Is that what ails ya? Again? That man ought to know when it's time to keep his hands to hisself."

"He never has," Louisa says.

"I can see it in ya, and you wantin' to be rid of it."

"Cain't do it again," Louisa answers, and Miss Lettie looks up from her fine, even stitches.

"You already got rid of one."

Anger boils up in Louisa at the damning, accusatory tone Lettie takes with her.

"He was too early."

But Louisa had walked along the snow-covered riverbank, unconcerned that she labored ahead of her time, her soft, worn belly barely bulging. She had walked and walked, silent, pained, and stubborn, until she squatted, grunted, and the child was born without life. She had tended to herself, swaddled the tiny boy, and tucked him into her coat. She climbed the hill to the blacktop, and walked to the old bridge across Coal River before turning up a rutted dirt road. At the top of the road was a small clearing before the mountain ascended again. There were a dozen or so hand dug mines on that mountain, some of them furrowed quite deep into the earth, and always there were ventilation shafts haphazardly dug on the other end, most of them full of water. Louisa stood on the edge of one such shaft for a long time, long enough for her feet to go numb before she dropped her son into the deep, cold water.

No one had known, except this hag, her two bottom teeth missing, one of her daughters a whore who sucks down whisky with those who seek her favors and come away with her filth. Far be it for Miss Lettie to stand in judgment, but she does, and she enjoys it. She enjoys it even more when it's the

8

more well-off ladies who seek her out, those who have heard of her gift with herbs and how they can get rid of things they don't want.

Miss Lettie sticks the needle in the quilt and stands, her own housedress as threadbare as Louisa's, large sweat stains spreading out from the armpits. Louisa can feel her own sweat trickling down her spine. Even the skin on her arms is moist. Miss Lettie opens a canister on the counter and from it hands Louisa a bag made of thin cheesecloth bulging at odd angles. A pungent, bitter smell wafts into the still, humid air.

"Boil your water and let it steep for at least ten minutes. If you don't start bleeding in three days, come back for more. After that, ain't gonna work. Have to deal with it."

Louisa murmurs her thanks, and Miss Lettie shrugs and reminds her she's not the first and she won't be the last.

"And I'd be tellin' that husband of yurn to keep his tallywacker to hisself."

Louisa pauses on the threshold as though to answer but doesn't.

That night she feigns sleep and rolls away when her husband reaches for her. She lays on the edge of the bed, stiff, her eyes blinking against the darkness. He rubs against her, his hands pulling at her sweaty nightgown.

"Quit!" Louisa pushes against his hand, "It's my time."

"Bullshit, woman. It's always your time now."

"Cain't do anymore babies. Cain't take care of the ones we got. Now, leave off!"

Arlie flops back to the bed stuffing his pillow under his head. He twitches his foot faster and faster until he explodes off of the bed and stalks away.

Louisa rises onto one arm as the front door slams. She stays that way for a while, listening, before dropping back to the bed. Curling onto her side, she picks at the mattress.

In the next room, the communal room for the children, sixteen-year-old Floyd throws his legs over the window frame and drops to the ground. In his pocket is a small sliver of soap, and he goes toward the river. His father, he knows, sits in his normal place on their stoop with a bottle of hooch between his feet. Floyd heard his mother, and he doesn't want to stay for what will follow. Besides, he has a date with Miss Lettie's youngest daughter, Wanda. She's really Miss Lettie's granddaughter, a cast off from one of her daughters who didn't want the responsibility. Floyd strips and dips into the water, washing the dust, sweat, and stench away.

He doesn't lie to himself, she's a whore, but she and her "boyfriend," Bill Mullins, were off again, and she always sulks around looking for someone to help make him jealous enough to slither back to her. Floyd doesn't care if Bill gets jealous or not. He just knows she's easy and he's hard. She rubbed herself all over him while they were swimming, even put her hand inside his shorts and stroked him until he had to shove her away and dive into the deep water while his sister, Lydia, sat watching them from the riverbank.

Lydia is ten months younger than Floyd, Irish twins they call them, and she had been wide awake as he slipped from the window. As the oldest girl, she is the only one afforded a cot in the bedroom. Two of her younger sisters, Doris and Donna, sleep on mattresses on the floor beside her. When she hears the door open, she turns onto her side toward the window, wishing she had slipped away as well. She lays very still, her head cocked so she can see the rising moon. She hears her father mutter, his feet shuffling between the mattresses, every sound amplified in the stillness – the squeak as his knee bends the mattress, the rustle of clothing, another squeak as the other knee hits a spring, the slurp as he licks his fingers (*it's what he does*), and Doris cries a little.

"Aaaay, aaaay, aaaay," but Doris cries like that all the time. All of her moods are punctuated by that sound, and she cries again as Arlie grunts. The mattress squeaks a steady rhythm. Lydia shuts her eyes tight.

Squeak, squeak, aaaay, squeak, squeak, squeak, aaaay

"What is daddy doing to Doris?" Donna asked her one day as they hung clothes to dry. Lydia shook out a shirt and put the pins on the neck so it dried flat.

"Don't matter," Lydia answered, "Just don't let him do it to you, okay?"

Donna nodded and stuck another pin on the line.

"Do you think Mama's gonna send Doris to that hospital?" Every so often Louisa got mad enough to talk about sending Doris away. It had gone on as long as Lydia could remember, and she scraped her sweaty bangs to one side and looked at the listing little shanty and the squalor, their dusty bare feet, and the faded clothes on the line.

"No, Daddy won't let her, but she'd be better off away from this fuckhole."

"You ain't supposed to say that word!"

"I don't care. That's what this is."

Arlie grunts twice and exhales. Lydia opens her eyes and thinks, I have to get out of here.

Wanda shrugs into her shirt. She and Floyd had gone at it twice and he'd lasted long enough the second time that she enjoyed it. He would never measure up to Bill, but no one ever would. Floyd is good looking and he is gentler than some of the other boys, even Bill, and even though she has a reputation, he doesn't act like it. He treats her sort of like a girlfriend. He puts his pants on and throws a stick onto the fire.

When she asks if he's going back, he shakes his head.

"Just gonna lay here and hope the bugs don't eat me up. Too hot to sleep at my house."

"Mine too."

11

Floyd doesn't look at her. He snaps another branch and feeds the fire. They are a half of a mile from the shanties, cossetted on a flat above the river. The dark woods and bottomland know their feet as well as they know the landscape. A brief cool breeze trickles out of the hollow and Wanda exhales and folds her legs under her as she drops beside him. She picks a blade of grass and twirls it between her fingers. She wants to lean against him but they are sweaty and sticky to the point of discomfort. She was surprised when he showed up, fresh washed even. She had been angry that afternoon and got him horny because she could, and she had made the date with him because she could, and she had fucked him because she could. She fools herself into thinking Miss Lettie doesn't know where she is or what she's doing, but Miss Lettie knows everything. Miss Lettie knows she's with the Belcher boy, and she knows what they're doing, and like everyone else in Down Johns, she's too damn tired to care.

Wanda lays back, her head cradled on her arm, and Floyd lies beside her. The fire smolders causing thick smoke to drift over them, stinging their eyes. Floyd waves the smoke away from his face.

"You ever think of leaving here," she asks.

"All the time."

Lydia isn't sure where she's going or how she's going to get there, but she drops out of the window anyway. Her shoes are too tight and her brassiere is too loose, a hand-me-down from her mother. The skirt is her best. It is also hot and much longer than the mini-skirts that the richer girls were wearing at school, and her shirt is also her best but faded and a bit threadbare. One of her cousins works in the city. She washes bedclothes and towels at a hotel. She says it is better than being stuck up the holler, and Lydia figures anything is better than Down Johns.

But when she crests the bank and steps onto the berm, everything familiar looks different. The trees hang over the narrow road casting deceptive shadows and although the night is devoid of human noises, it is full of night sounds, crickets, and bullfrogs, and a hoot owl calls from across the river. She wipes her palms on her skirt and starts toward the bridge. Even though the sound of a car would carry, she looks over her shoulder every few feet as though there is one sneaking up on her.

She reaches the bridge, and as all are want to do, she leans over the edge to stare at the inky water. There's a campfire, probably someone gigging frogs. She hears the faint drone of an engine and notices light shining on her legs. The car is sleek and what light there is reflects off of the shiny chrome bumper.

Lydia steps up and sticks her thumb out. She shouldn't, she knows, as well as she knows who's driving the cherry red 1961 Chevy Impala Super Sport. Its owner, Bill Mullins, was showing it off one day in the school parking lot for his brothers, Davy and Everett, who was nicknamed Grim. Everyone was talking about it, repeating every detail over and over and burning it into her head. But, no one talked about what he uses that car for – bootlegging moonshine. Everyone knows he runs into Kentucky, sometimes as far as Louisville, a world away. The car slows, stops, and Lydia flinches when Bill revs the engine. All of the windows are down and Bill's hair curls wild and black against itself.

"Where ya goin', pretty lady?" Lydia inhales, the silkiness of his voice startles her. She had expected it to be rough and cruel, and she doesn't know how to answer his question so she shrugs.

"I don't know. Away from here I guess."

"Do you wanna ride or not?" He sounds bemused and maybe a little irritated, "I got somewhere to be."

As an answer, Lydia opens the door and gets in. As she shuts the door, Bill revs the engine twice, pulses the clutch, squeals the tires, and fishtails across the bridge. Lydia grips the door handle but doesn't gasp or cry out or act frightened. Bill smirks.

"You live at Down Johns, right? Close to Wanda?"

"Yeah."

"Fuckin' shithole. Been tellin' her to get out of there, but she's scared. Big fuckin' baby. She ain't got the guts to run away. That's what you're doin' ain't it, Lydia?"

"How you know my name?" It scares her. Bill knowing her name makes her heart pound against her chest, she is sure he can hear it, but he can't. He can see her heartbeat though, he sees it in the side of her neck, he sees it in her wide eyes, he knows they are so blue they look silver, and she is equal parts courage and fear. He knows Wanda has been sniffing around Lydia's brother, hell, she's probably already fucked him, and he doesn't really care. He knows Lydia comes from nothing and has nothing, and he knows she's afraid it will always be that way, and she's more afraid of that than anything else, even him. He feels it in her. He likes it.

"I know people," he answers, "That all you takin' with ya?" He points at the small bundle in her lap.

"Yeah."

"You got any money?"

"No."

"How you think you're gonna eat?"

Lydia shrugs, "I've gone hungry before. I ain't afraid of it."

She is becoming defensive, and Bill talks about other things, school, the upcoming Fourth of July parade, and she relaxes. When he turns off of the main road, she looks at him and asks where they are going, more with curiosity than fear.

"I told you I had somewhere to be. Just stay in the car and don't say anything, okay?"

"We goin' to pick up the 'shine?"

Bill pulls the car onto a second road, shuts the engine off, and turns toward her.

"I already have my shine," he says, "Now, I need my liquor."

He's warming me up, Lydia thinks, but still, she is flattered. He is much different than she had imagined, but she

14

also does not know if it is him or just flattery, just the warm up to ask for, or to take, something more. She knows what is coming. It burns in her nipples and her pussy. She has already lost her virginity. It was awkward and otherwise nothing to speak of and she is not afraid to have sex with Bill. Maybe he has a better idea of what he is doing than Clay did. Lydia knows there is a price. There is always a price. She has lain awake enough nights to know the price her mother paid, and then poor Doris. Women always pay with sex. Lydia turns in the seat, lifting and sliding her foot under her, exposing her leg a little more. The waning moon shines through the windshield, enough that she can see his eyes wander to her leg, then his hand, his fingertips stroking her thigh.

"Cain't be doin' that right now," Bill says, and raises up and adjusts his jeans as headlights shine into the car, "Stay here."

They race through the night around switchbacks and roads so narrow and steep when she looks out the side window it's like she's flying into darkness. She is, she knows, hurtling toward something. It's thrilling and frightening. She's being reborn. Where has this life been? What is this life with the wind whipping through open windows, rutted roads, and black-haired wicked saviors? She wants this life. She wants this freedom.

Wanda jerks awake. She was dreaming, dreaming of falling. The moon is higher, the stars have moved, and the fire burns low, the coals deep orange. A mosquito whines in her ear and she swats at it as she pokes the fire with a branch. Blue flames lick up and she throws the branch onto the coals causing sparks to erupt into the night.

Something stirs within her and has been for the past two weeks. She has waited for her woman time and the time has stretched further and thinner and thinner, and like her grandmother, there are things she knows, most she does not want to know. She knows there is a baby rooting in her womb,

15

a dark-haired son or daughter (a daughter, she knows, but won't admit). Bill does not want her, he wants the scratch to his itch, her convenience, her compliance, which he loves as much as he hates it, as much as he hates her clinginess and her weakness and fear. He wants her out of Down Johns, but won't take her with him. These are things she knows that she wishes she did not know, things she is too young to know and too stubborn to accept. She will never accept the things to come.

Bill stands at the night window of a run-down motel. It is two a.m. but the clerk has been waiting for him. He is paid well for his cooperation.

"Seven dollars," he says.

"I'll need it for a week," Bill answers and slides a fifty through the slot. When the clerk raises his eyebrows, Bill stares at him without explanation and the man makes the change.

Lydia jerks awake. She was dreaming, dreaming of falling. Bill's arm lies over her hip, she feels his breath on her shoulder, his coarse chest hair tickles her back. He did have a much better idea of what he was doing than Clay. He had poured her a bit of 'shine, just enough to cover the bottom of the plastic cup.

"Don't need that," she said. Bill smiled and offered it again.

"Won't hurt nothin' though, will it?" The fumes made her eyes water, it burned going down, and she coughed and sipped again. The 'shine exploded in her head like fireworks, her eyes crossed, and she put her hand on the bed to steady herself. Bill took the cup away from her.

"Easy now," he laughed, "You'll be sick drinkin' like that on an empty stomach. Ole Stimey should have us a burger here in a minute."

People did what Bill wanted, whether he paid them or they were afraid, people answered to him. At two-twenty,

Stimey delivered two burgers with a handful of potato chips, and even after she had eaten, Lydia was still flying, flying and falling into darkness.

Bill peels off a hundred dollars in twenty dollar bills and hands them to Lydia. She has never held more than a few coins.

"I ain't leavin' you here with nothin'. I'll be back next Saturday."

Lydia stays seated on the edge of the bed, the bills moist in her hand. She had been too surprised to question him, as though she believes it would make a difference. She locks the door and goes to the bathroom. She puts the bills on top of the toilet. It takes her a few minutes to figure out the shower, but not before she douses her downturned head in cold water. She has only ever bathed in a washtub in already used bathwater. She adjusts the heat and the spray and steps in, turning and turning, ducking under the water again and again. She is fascinated by the little shampoo bottle and the little bar of soap. Lord, that bar of soap would last them a month. She wraps herself in the biggest towel and sits again on the edge of the bed feeling cleaner than she ever has.

"Where's Lydia?" Louisa asks as she spoons oatmeal into Donna's bowl.

Donna wants to say the f-word, as she just recently learned what it really means and how to use it properly. She wants to tell her mother that Lydia left after her daddy finished fucking Doris, because that's what it was.

"She left after Daddy finished with Doris."

Louisa's hand stops mid-air and a dollop of oatmeal drips onto the table. She throws the spoon down and slaps Donna. Floyd flinches as Donna gasps and starts crying. The three youngest boys pause in the doorway, and the baby, Beth, stops banging her spoon on the highchair.

"Aaaaaay. Aaaaaay," Doris reaches for the oatmeal spoon and Louisa smacks her hand again and again, then her face and tender ears until Doris screams.

"Mom!" Floyd jumps up, "Stop!"

"What in the Sam Hell is going on?" Arlie comes out of the bedroom bare-chested. Louisa whirls and lifts her chin.

"Lydia ran away."

Arlie scratches his chest and looks around, not at anyone, just anywhere but Louisa.

"Well," he shrugs, "One less mouth to feed."

Wanda and Floyd lie by the river. It's been three weeks since their first time, mere minutes since their last and when Wanda sits up and tells him her woman time is late, Floyd stays sprawled on the ground.

Wanda tried to talk to Bill, but his cousin, Jake, told her he'd been staying in Louisville a lot. She picked up bottles beside the road to get the money to call him from the pay phone at the post office. He was never home, and it was not finally she who tracked him down, but he who tracked her down as she walked along the road on her way to call him again. She got into the car and he drove them onto the mountain near where Lydia and Floyd's brother lie in his grave. A chill passed over her as he parked the car, and she was afraid.

"Stop harassing my family, Wanda. If I wanted ya, I'd come and get ya."

Wanda huffed and told him she was late.

"I know ya knocked up, just not sure it's mine. (But he did, he knew) And I don't want ya. (Itch, scratch, itch, scratch, that would always be true) I got better things goin' on, so stop your bullshit."

"You know it's yurn, William Lee!"

"I don't want *you*, Wanda! So leave off!"

She cried and begged, and not until he threatened to leave her on the mountain did she hush.

"They hirin' at the mine again," Floyd says, "Figure I ought to go down there and see about gettin' on."

"What are you talkin' 'bout?"

"Cain't support a family doing odd jobs, unless you want to raise up our baby here. Well, do ya? Do ya wanna raise up our baby here?"

Wanda shakes her head.

"Then I'll see about a job in the mines."

"We should get married."

Lydia looks at Bill's reflection in the mirror and finishes her ponytail before dropping her hands and turning to him.

"What for?" Lydia asks.

Her tone, her indifference, it pisses him off.

"Don't play dumb, Lydia. I know you're knocked up."

"Don't matter. I ain't keepin' it. Don't, Bill. I'm fifteen. What the hell do I need with a kid? So I can end up like my mom? Fuckin' PG all the time, broke down without a pot to piss in? No thanks."

"What? You think I'd let you live in Down Johns? You think I cain't take care of you?"

"Why do you even want to? You didn't even know me two months ago."

But he wants to know her. He's intrigued by her stubbornness and her strength. She has two jobs. She works mornings at a diner and afternoons cleaning rooms for Stimey. Stimey pays her a little more than the rent on the room, and the waitressing job feeds her. She is fearless. She doesn't need him. He hates it.

"Don't worry about it," she says, "I'm saving money, and I'll get through."

"Shit. They'll fire you as soon as your belly pops out."

Lydia shrugs, "Still got this place."

Bill stands up, pushes her against the wall, and braces his arms on either side of her.

"Only as long as I say so."

His face is so close his breath is on her cheek, but she tilts her head to look into his eyes and then ducks under his arm.

"I gotta go to work."

"Don't need ya anymore. You can get your pay when you turn in your uniform," the manager's wife says. She is waiting for Lydia by the back entrance, and her eyes skip to Lydia's stomach. As soon as Lydia's foot hits the sidewalk in front of the hotel, Stimey bangs on the window and motions her over. Goddamn.

"Hey, uh, we won't be needing you anymore, uh, and uh," he looks pained, "but I'll let ya stay up through next week, no charge. Just don't tell anybody, okay? And uh, I'm sorry, okay? I am." Lydia nods.

Bill leans in the open doorway of the room, his arms crossed over his chest. She stops in front of him.

"Only as long as I say so, Lydia."

"You're a cocksucker."

Bill buys her a new suit for their wedding, light pink, a pillbox hat with a veil, white gloves, and white pumps. Lydia wears hosiery for the first time. She lies about her age and no one questions her. It is simple and it is very possible the justice of the peace is drunk on moonshine. Then, she meets the family.

Bill is the third oldest of fourteen children. His youngest sister, Josie, who is six, has nieces and nephews older than she is. As Lydia soon discovers, she is an odd child, but not as odd as some of them are, nor as some of them will become, even her own children. Theirs is a life steeped in the "old ways," superstitions, old wives' tales, folklore, strange

20

occurrences, strange stories, and strange ways. And it is Josie who begins this odd journey for her, the journey into the heart of this family, when she sits on her brother's lap, which Lydia is told later is odd in itself as Josie does not like her brother, and says to him,

"She's smarter than you."

Bill laughs and asks why she would say such a thing.

"Because she knows you only want what you cain't have."

Those within earshot look first at Josie and Bill, then at Lydia with a mixture of mirth and knowing. Bill laughs the loudest, but he puts his sister off of his lap and swats her on the butt hard enough to make her frown. For the rest of the day, Lydia turns to find him staring at her, and not with the gentleness of a new husband, but as someone who has been beaten at his own game, someone who isn't sure if he's angry or grudgingly proud.

"You played me," he says as soon as they get in the car. Lydia leans back against the seat and crosses her arms.

"Just don't think it's because I love ya and I cain't live without ya. I ain't livin' in filth for the rest of my life. It was your dumb luck to come drivin' down the road. It was my luck you cain't keep your hands to yourself, and you're so goddamn stuck on yourself ya think ever' woman ought to marry ya, or at least want to. You did the rest."

Bill laughs. He hates her. He loves her.

They do not go back to Louisville. Bill wants her close to his family, so they move into a small house that once belonged to his eldest brother not more than a mile from the homestead. Lydia argues with him, but he reminds her she can go to Down Johns if she is unhappy.

Wanda stands in line at the gas station. It is the only place close enough to get a cold grape Nehi. She and Floyd moved to a little house with three rooms and an outhouse. It was out of Down Johns, but one could hardly pretend that Maxine's Ridge was very much of a step up. Floyd got on at the mines, but the money is slow coming in, or so Floyd says. She does not read very well so he pays the bills himself, and he gives her enough for cigarettes and a pop. Wanda shifts from foot to foot as Jake makes change for the man in front of her. Floyd fussed at her earlier for not wearing the shoes he bought for her, but, as is their way, she is saving them for when she needs them. The man finishes and Wanda tells Jake what she wants. He turns and gets the Nehi from the cooler and sets it on the counter along with a pack of generic cigarettes.

"Kind of funny, ain't it?" he asks.

"What's funny?"

"You and Floyd gettin' married, and his sister marryin' Bill. Never would've thought it."

Wanda is suddenly dizzy, and she grabs the edge of the counter. She can't swallow, she can't breathe. She can feel every grain of grit under her feet and the smell of oil from the dark splotches on the floor overwhelms her. She can hear Jake asking if she is okay, but she can't answer. Then she is sitting on a pile of tires but she can't remember how she got there, and Jake is pushing her head between her knees. She realizes she is shaking and her body is running with cold sweat. She wants to vomit, and she does, nothing much but bile.

Jake takes her home, saving her a long walk in the hot sun, and she cries and apologizes, but Jakes feels as though it is he who should apologize. Instead, he hands her the cigarettes and the grape Nehi and leaves her on her doorstep.

"I told ya to drink the tea, now, live with it," Miss Lettie says, "Don't matter though, if ya don't stop snottin' around, you'll lose that baby anyway. Ya oughta be grateful Floyd married ya, so quit ya whinin'."

It's true. Wanda started having pains and a little bleeding after she cried and cried, telling Floyd it's what women in the family way do, then she got scared because the baby is Bill's, and she wants it. So, she quit crying. Didn't do any good anyway.

22

Lydia pulls into a parking spot at the grocery store. That was one thing she insisted on, learning to drive. Driving meant independence and freedom, and it also meant she could make her own liquor runs, which her father-in-law, Victor, has allowed her to do on occasion. When she makes the run, she gets the cut. Victor likes her so well he nicknames her Bonnie, "Bonnie Parker Mullins," he says. Bill just shakes his head. It wouldn't do him any good to say something because his family is just like he is. If he didn't teach her to drive, someone else would. His sisters dote on her. Right now she's wearing hand-me-down maternity clothes, but they are as pristine as the day they were bought. It is very noticeable now that she is pregnant. Just a few more months, and she will be a mother, and she is still not sure how she feels.

Before she can open the door and step out into the January gloom, she sees another woman, heavily pregnant, leave the grocery store. It is her mother, and Lydia is ashamed. She is ashamed of her mother, and she is ashamed of herself for feeling the way she does. Her mother looks old, tired, and bitter. She knows about Floyd and Wanda, but Donna hasn't offered this piece of information. Lydia sends her money and every Saturday Donna calls her from the gas station. She wants to offer her mother a ride, at least, some small part of her does, but Lydia watches her walk away.

"Why didn't you tell me about Mama?"

"Would it make any damn difference? She takes all the money you send and I still don't have shoes for school. Why cain't you let me come and live with you and Bill? I'll help you with the baby."

It is the same argument they have every time they talk. Regardless of what Donna says, she would still be Lydia's responsibility, and Lydia doesn't want her.

In February, a seventh daughter is stillborn to Arlie and Louisa Belcher. They name her Helen Mae, and she is buried beside her sisters.

In March, a first daughter is born to Bill Mullins. Her name is Rosa Lee.

In April, a second daughter is born to Bill Mullins. Her name is Jessie Lee.

Lydia cups her daughter's head as she nurses, smoothing the black hair on her tiny head. Lydia inhales her sweet baby scent. Jessie blinks at her with slate blue eyes that will very soon lighten to a startling silver blue like her mother's. Lydia's mother-in-law, Astoria, and her sister-in-law, Eleanor, hover nearby. Now she understands why Bill wanted them close to the homestead, or perhaps it really wasn't his intention to have his mother and sisters and sisters-in-law at his house all the time. There is always someone to offer advice about breastfeeding or a salve for her sore, cracked nipples, and Eleanor had driven her the three hours to a clinic in Louisville for the Pill.

"You don't want another one too soon," Eleanor had said, "Just make sure you take it every day, and don't tell Mama. She may want a dozen or more, but I'll be happy with two or three."

Lydia is content for now with her precious daughter, the one she thought she didn't want, but who has become the center of her world. Even Bill, as taciturn as he could be, is enthralled, not just with his baby girl and the way she looks at him, and as she grows, her gummy smile and belly laughs, but also his wife and the gentleness of her stroking hands as she nurses, her smile as she kisses Jessie's fingers as they reach for her face. She is a woman in love.

Lydia, elbow deep in dishwater, watches rain slash the window. The giant oak outside the window, its leaves rusty red, heaves in the wind. The radio is turned low as Jessie sleeps, the heat from the stove warms the kitchen, the smell of baking bread, Bill's favorite, fills the house. There is a light knock at the door and Astoria lets herself in the house. She shakes her coat out and takes off her rain bonnet.

"I always thought October rain was the chilliest. My, that bread smells delicious." She pours herself a cup of coffee, sits down at the kitchen table, and takes out her knitting. Astoria won't stay long, they will chat, she will kiss the baby, then she will make her rounds to her other close family and friends. It is her way. Today, however, she stays until the bread is cool enough to cut, unable to resist it. They slather it in butter and Astoria's black raspberry jam, a decadent afternoon treat.

Lydia stands at the door with Jessie on her hip as Astoria ties her rain bonnet on and kisses them both on the cheek. When Lydia opens the door, Jake is on her doorstep, and behind him is Donna. Lydia pushes open the screen door.

"Come in, come in out of the rain. Donna? Honey, what's wrong?" Lydia asks as Donna clings to her.

"I'm sorry to have to tell you, Lydia, but your sister, Doris, died. Donna asked that I bring her up here," Jake answers.

"Oh, my goodness," Astoria says, and unties her rain bonnet.

"What happened?" It could be a dozen things. Doris was sickly, she had breathing problems, she choked on food a lot, she was clumsy.

"I'm not certain, ma'am."

"Thank you for bringing Donna to us," Astoria says, "Thank you so much, Jake, for letting us know. You best be gettin' back to work," and that is how Astoria gets rid of him. Donna pushes away from Lydia.

"Mama let her die. She was too ashamed to take her to the doctor. She died from the fever."

"That don't make any sense, Donna."

"She smelled, she smelled like death on the side of the road, and that's the way Mama treated her! She cried, Lydia!

25

She suffered! I begged Mama to help her, and that son of a bitch was afraid, afraid they'd know it was him that did it!"

Lydia loses her breath. She feels dizzy and sick and sits down on the couch. She presses her lips into Jessie's head, holds them there, and closes her eyes.

"Did what, Donna?" Astoria asks. Donna startles as though she has just realized Astoria is there. She looks at Lydia, but Lydia won't look at her.

"Doris had a baby," Donna whispers, "I think she did anyway. I mean, not like your baby, just a lump of stuff, and they buried it by the river so nobody would know. But Doris got sick, she got the fever, and after a while, she smelled like she was already dead. She was so sick, Lydia. She cried and cried, until she just couldn't no more."

"Shut up," Lydia says, "shut up before I lose my mind!"

"You? You think you're gonna lose your mind? You bitch! You weren't there! You left us!" Donna drags her dirty cuffs over her eyes and her face. It smears the snot running from her nose, her eyes swollen and callous, "You left *me*."

The house is quiet other than the sound of rain on the roof. Eleanor sits with Lydia at the kitchen table, the coffee cups from earlier still sit in the cold dishwater. Lydia's eyes burn every time she blinks and a dull headache radiates from her temples. She sees a flash of light as someone pulls into the driveway.

"It looks like Bill's home. I'm gonna go, honey. You just let me know if you need anything." Lydia hears them talking, too low for her to hear. Bill comes into the kitchen and pulls a chair over to sit close to her. He covers her hands with his.

"That church Floyd goes to, they're gonna bury her." Lydia stares at the table, her bottom lip quivering.

"What church?"

Bill shrugs, "That Pentacostal place up Maxine's Ridge. It's gonna be quick, too. They'll be sittin' up with her tomorrow night."

"What are the police gonna do?"

"Nothin' that I know of. Police weren't there. Old Doc Mooney signed the death certificate and that was it." But that wasn't going to be *it*.

"Donna's at your mama's," Lydia says.

"I know, and I think it's best that she stay there. I ain't sayin' she cain't live here. I just think it's best that she don't. Mama lost three more babies after Josie. That's what makes her happy, taking care of family."

He doesn't say it will make her unhappy. She's a good mother. If Jessie is her sunshine, he is her moon, and that's the way he wants it to stay.

"Mama and Eleanor will go with you and Donna tomorrow. Grim and I have to go to Louisville."

Lydia prefers that no one goes, but she also knows this is a fight she will not win.

They choose seats toward the back of the church. Jessie is asleep on Lydia's shoulder and Lydia rearranges the blanket over her head, anything to keep from looking at the simple wooden coffin. If she sees her mother cry, she may scream. Donna sits between Lydia and Astoria. We're too young for this, Lydia thinks, we're too young.

Jessie begins rooting, arousing from sleep, ascending from her dreams. There is a shuffling, the edge of a coat brushes against her head disturbing the blanket, and Jessie raises her head and looks up into the eyes of her Uncle Floyd. Were it not for her eyes, Floyd would swear he was looking at his own daughter. But she is beside him on her mother's lap, and when he looks at his wife, she is staring at Jessie. He wanted to believe Rose was his. Wanda has dark hair. Wanda has brown eyes. Rose takes after her mother. That's all.

Lydia turns her head and sees Rose. Rose's eyes are dark, her hair full of soft, black curls, a pug nose, the spitting

27

image of her father. Dear God. Lydia sees her brother's face and moves Jessie to her lap. She offers nothing. It is as though she has never belonged to this other family. Eleanor takes her hand and squeezes it. Lydia hands Jessie to her and stands. She walks down the aisle toward the wooden coffin and her parents. Her youngest sister, Beth, hides in her mother's skirt until she sees Lydia.

"Lissie! Lissie!"

Lydia slings Beth onto her hip, and before her mother can speak, Lydia says,

"I'm giving you what you want. I'm taking Beth and Donna, and if you try to stop me, I'll tell. I'll tell what you did, and I'll tell what he did."

"I did the best I could!"

"You're pathetic."

Lydia walks back down the aisle.

"We're leaving," she says. Floyd looks at the floor and Wanda stares straight ahead. Rose is the only one to watch them go.

Bill returns early the next morning. Lydia sits on the couch while Jessie plays with her feet on a blanket on the floor. Bill kneels down and rubs her belly, making her laugh.

"How did it go?" he asks.

"I saw your other daughter," Lydia says, "She looks well enough."

Bill sits back on his heels, lowers his head, and sighs.

Wanda wrings out diapers in the sink and drapes them over the back of the dining room chair to dry in front of the stove. She looks around and realizes she left the washbasin in the bedroom. When she gets to the doorway, she sees Floyd standing at the foot of the bed, his hands in his pockets, looking down at Rose as she naps.

"What are you doin'?"

Floyd drops his head and rocks back on his heels.

"Wishin' she was mine."

29

The Fruit of a Christian

My inability to keep my mouth shut started early on in my life, and most often it happened in church. My dad's parents were higher ups at Tinney's Branch Freewill Baptist Church (Amen). That there is an oxymoron, because they ain't nothing freewillin' about being a Baptist. I spent a lot of time sitting up straight and following along in my "Precious Child and Holy Hymns of the Baptist, and All Others Shall Rot in Hell, Especially Catholics" book which was guaranteed to force feed Christian ideologies as surely as squeezing my nose together would make me open my mouth.

Trouble was, I didn't exactly agree with all the things my holy hymnal said. I wasn't really sure what was wrong with Catholics, other than they were allowed to drink wine (but so had Jesus), but my Mamaw called them a bunch of drunks and made my Papaw stop drinking his Pabst Blue Ribbon. I'm still not sure if the greater sin was drinking beer, or drinking Pabst. God will have to figure that out for me.

There was something else, too. My Sunday School teacher lived down the road from me, and she probably figured I was judgment on my parents for their Godless ways. She might have wondered a time or two if I was some kind of tribulation for her own sins. It may have been the way I narrowed my eyes at her when she said if you keep sinning, then God isn't going to like you anymore. That's not what I had read in the Bible, or at least what I thought I read, so I asked someone who wasn't going to immediately start praying for my salvation - my mother.

Loretta Mullins King tapped the ash off the end of her generic cigarette, the same ash I thought was going to fall into the bowl of generic oatmeal she was stirring, it had happened before, and told me the Freewheelers didn't believe in everlasting salvation. If you sinned and sinned and sinned, eventually God was going to get tired of you and condemn you to hell anyway. Now, if that ain't an example of God's grace, I don't know what is. What a damn Indian giver!

It didn't do much good to ask my Sunday School teacher questions either. I was confused about why dinosaurs weren't in the Bible, and whether or not Noah had them on the ark, and who did Adam's and Eve's kids marry, because marrying your brother is gross. She gave me a stern look and started reeling off scripture like a square dance caller . . . "And Jesus said, if you think they hate you, well by God, they hated me first, now step to your left and promenade." That scripture would lead to me holding the distinction for the best interruption of a church service, one I held for almost fourteen years.

It was John 15, and I'm pretty sure it was close to Easter because it was one of the lessons Jesus taught the Disciples before the Romans crucified Him, although, to be honest, I was always told it was the Jews who killed Jesus, which I thought was just fucking dumb considering he was King of the damn Jews to start with! And Pontius Pilate wasn't a Jew, he was a Roman. Don't ever point this out to the fundies. They'll just say the Jews handed Jesus over, and that was the same thing. Then ask them who would have died for their sins if Jesus hadn't done it and watch their eyes roll back in their head. Hahahahaha!

Anywho. . .

That was our Sunday School lesson, the fruit of a Christian, that's what John 15 is all about, letting God prune the sin away from ya and you bearing fruit as a Christian. All I could imagine were peach trees, and I'm not sure why we were peaches instead of apples since I'd never even seen a peach tree, but peaches are my favorite fruit, so I imagined all of us Christians as peach trees, and God just snipping away at all of our sin. All I really accomplished by doing that was making myself hungry.

Now, I normally was home sitting on my butt watching Nova on public television during evening Sunday service, but it must have been Easter break because that fateful Sunday I was sitting smack dab on the front pew as Brother Fleetwood took to the pulpit. Brother Fleetwood could get a good one going. He used some sort of hair stuff that gave him a flattened Oral Roberts look, but if he moved around too much that hair stuff would feel the spirit and leave Brother Fleetwood brushing his greasy hair out of his eyes like a convict on a chain gang.

Brother Fleetwood didn't just move out from behind the pulpit, oh no, Brother Fleetwood took to the floor, right in front of yours truly. There were two steps leading from the floor to the pulpit, and he spent at least half an hour on each one before staggering my way, kicking the tires and lighting the fires of brimstone and sal-VA-tion!

He asked, no less than half a dozen times, what the fruit of a Christian was. The Oral Roberts gel had seen the light and sweat and Brother Fleetwood is holding his hands out in front of him, shaking and baking with the power of the Holy Ghost, preachin' and praisin', and irritating the shit out of me. I mean, the man was standing right in front of me, pounding his fist, agitating like a washer, red-faced, sweat dripping, bellowing like an auctioneer at the Pearly Gates.

"Now, I wanna know, I wanna know, what is the fruit of a Christian? The Bible says you must bear fruit. We are the fruit of Jeeeeesus. You have been chosen by Jeeeeesus to bear fruit, and I wanna know what is the fruit of a Christian. And Jeeeesus said to love each other as I have loved you! Now, I wanna know *what is the fruit of Christian*!"

I figured no one else had paid attention in Sunday School and it was up to me to answer him so he would shut the hell up and stop spraying sweat and spit all over me.

"Another Christian!"

That shut him up all right, and everyone else too. His jaw dropped, and for a second I thought drool was going to drip out of his mouth right onto the floor. He looked like a wet, confused balloon that had just been pricked by a pin, and I had no choice but to stare back at him and wonder if my Mamaw was going to knuckle me in the back of the head.

"Amen."

My Papaw saved me by saying that simple word, and a

smattering of "Amens" came from the congregation, and I didn't get knuckled in the back of the head. Now, word spread about what I'd said, and you'd thunk I was some kind of prophet. Even the Church of Godders, with their long hair and even longer skirts, patted me on the head at the Shop & Save, even though my hair was so short I was mistaken for a boy, and I was wearing pants.

I'd had enough of the Freewheelers though, so I cycled my way through the Church of Godders, short hair and all. I skipped the Pentacostals 'cause I figured they spoke in tongues because they were handling snakes. I know that's about the only way to get me to speak in tongues. I tried the Jehovah's Witnesses, the Methodists, and the Church of Christ. In the end, I went back to the family faith – The Old Ways.

Like I said, my speaking up in church was the stuff of legend for many years until Carlene Castleberry one-upped me. Seems she was sitting a few pews back one Sunday when the preacher asked for prayer requests. Now, you could do spoken or unspoken, and pretty much everyone already knew who you were praying for when you said "unspoken," like, "Hell, you all know my brother, Ray, is a drunk, just pray for him," and crazy enough, everyone prayed out loud. You didn't just bow your head and let the preacher pray for you and you move your lips like you cared about Aunt Maude's bad hip, no siree, you had to pray out loud so everyone knew you were serious.

Now, Carlene wasn't happy with an unspoken request, nope, she said it loud and proud.

"I'm requesting prayer for Melinda Elkins for sleeping with my husband."

I'm sure that would have caused a twitter all by itself, but since Melinda and her husband, John, were sitting right across the aisle from Carlene and her husband, Rick, it caused more than a twitter. It was a cat fight.

Melinda and Carlene stepped into the aisle and started throwing insults, then punches. The preacher, some new fella from a few counties over, waded in and commenced with the laying on of hands. I almost fell off the barstool when my cousin Thermy called to tell me about it. She wasn't there, she's a Church of Godder, but of course the fundie phone lines were jamming all over the hollers.

If you're going to be knocked off a pedestal, that's the way to go.

"Well," I said, "Jesus said, 'These things I command you, that ye loooooove one another.'"

"Virgie! You're going to hell."

I'll see ye sinners there.

Birdsong

Don Mullins takes up a stick, a stout, twisted piece of polished ironwood. It has a fat ninety-degree handle created by grapevines. He has other walking sticks, and although stout, the handles are straight and thin and make his knuckles ache. One of his great-granddaughters, he can't remember which, painted vines and flowers on the stick. He isn't given to pretty things, but he likes that piece of ironwood.

In his other hand he holds a book by Louis L'Amour. He hasn't bothered to read to the title. What books he owns he's read dozens of times. Sometimes he finds a new title at a yard sale, but mainly he sticks to the aged, yellowing, musty books on his bookshelf. Their covers are tattered, some have been mended with masking tape, the pages dirty and warped by water, the spines broken and creased. He shuts the door to his house without locking it, forgetting again that his wife passed the year before and is not there to watch over their home.

He picks up the minnow bucket from its normal place outside the door and shuffles down the concrete walkway that winds around his stucco house. The white stucco had been poorly applied and crumbles in giant patches revealing the simple block and mortar construction underneath. The faded green awnings over the windows are the same ones that have been on the house since he bought it sixty years ago. After constructing the breezeway cover, he hadn't felt the need to remove the awnings. Work for nothing.

His brother, Victor, and his boy, Bill, like to come by and sit on Don's front porch, watch the river, and gossip. When others in the neighborhood, or just driving by, notice them on the porch, they stop too, anxious to hear their stories of stills and moonshine and fast cars. On those days, Don sits in his lawn chair, the old kind with wooden arms and wide woven strips fraying into bristly hues of orange, green, and tan. He crosses his hairy arms over his bulbous belly pregnant with bacon fat, fried eggs, and age, gray chest hair sprouting from the "V" in his shirt. On cold days he wears a blue plaid shirt with the cuffs unbuttoned which is as faded as the chair and the awning and has a dark blue patch on the elbow of the right sleeve. On very cold days he sits in a cracked faux leather chair that bleeds tan stuffing and carries a permanent indentation of his body, a Louis L'Amour book spread-eagle on his belly. The chair sits just inside the glass front door so he can still see the river. Before his wife, Lou, had passed, she sat opposite him on a barstool, drank coffee, and smoked unfiltered Camels.

A blue haze often drifted near the ceiling and Don concentrated on the wisp of smoke emanating from the fire tip or the yellow nicotine and black crescent burn marks along the edge of the silver sparkled Formica instead of Lou's shrill voice. His eyes slid away to the dozens of trinkets - salt and pepper shakers, thimbles, baby spoons, and decorative dishes from exotic locales like Florida and the Blue Ridge Mountains, all dulled with a layer of grease and tackiness. They fought for space among the fuzzy caterpillars of dust which lay motionless along the edges of the shelves. Spiders' webs hung like charms from the edge of the tarnished brass light fixture. Sometimes he caught the earthy aroma of ginseng drying on yesterday's newspaper. He grunted during pauses in her long soliloquies about everything from the day's gossip to the laziness of the nurses in the hospital where his sister had died.

It wasn't that he hadn't loved Lou, he had, and he still does. He had just loved her more when he was away. There was always something to do – mushrooms to find, ginseng to dig, fish to catch, deer to hunt, and frogs to gig. He had learned the secret of a long and happy marriage, and for him it was to spend as much time apart as possible and to turn his hearing aids down, which is why it is easy for him to believe that Lou is still alive.

It is cold, but not too cold. It hasn't frosted, and by the way the sun cracks over the mountain into the cloudless sky, Don surmises he will be removing his plaid shirt on the walk back from the minnow pool. Slow and methodical, his eyes constant on the western horizon, constant on the lookout for the massive coal trucks that rumble with such force his house shakes and the stucco crumbles, Don backs his truck onto the road and turns east into the sun. A half of a mile away, he turns right up Jenkins Road, and in another couple of miles he turns right onto Hardscrabble Road. His great-niece, Angeline, lives somewhere up the holler, but it's been so long since he's seen her, he doubts he would recognize her. He follows the road to where it forks.

The right hand fork dribbles down to a foot path. The left fork is a dead end at a mine gate that Don kicks every time he parks. Sometimes he urinates on it. When he was younger, there wasn't a gate, and he had taken his three boys hunting there, and on occasion, his entire family. Lou, his boys, his three daughters, and his grandchildren swarmed over the mountain to hunt mushrooms, hundreds of them. Then they retired to the crumbling stucco house and fried the mushrooms in cornmeal with trout and frog legs. Lord, those had been some good times.

He had made his living in the mines, but that was before they bought up the land and started putting up gates. He often ventures past this one, out of spite, just to see what he can see. There are still squirrels and mushrooms, but it just feels different.

Don kicks the gate, takes up the minnow bucket, the book, and a camouflage cushion and walks down the well-worn foot path. He figures the Donahue and Dotson boys use it as well. Minnows, hellgrammites, and night crawlers are free. He won't buy any of those over-priced Styrofoam containers full of half-dead bait that city people use.

There is a bend in the creek where the current has hollowed a deep hole in the bed. Don separates the inside bucket, pops the lid, and sits it in the creek. He turns and walks about fifteen steps away to the base of an oak tree. The roots are almost as accustomed to his girth as the faux leather chair, so much so the insides of the roots are worn smooth, first by his utilitarian gray pants, and now by the edges of the cushion.

It is a comfortable seat for a man, and he has seen a lot of wildlife pass before him, some he killed, but more often he allowed them to walk away unharmed. He found a bird book at a rummage sale and has spent a lot his time while sitting in the oak roots to figure out the different types of birds that sing from the brush. Some are easy – the brilliant red and dusty-red cardinals, blue jays, crows, house sparrows, and the screeching call of the red-tailed hawk. Some he discovered new names for – the little yellow bird was a goldfinch, the small black and white bird with the red head wasn't called a woodpecker, it was a yellow-bellied sapsucker, and one day he saw a cedar waxwing, but only once.

Between ten and eleven o'clock, the sun turned to hit the tree. Depending on the time of year, either the sun warmed him or the leaves staunched the sunlight and kept him cool. Always, Don slept. Lou never knew. What she thought was bad luck was Don not caring about killing anything anymore. He only cared about the birds singing, the squirrels racing and rolling through the leaves, the gentle murmurs and gurgles of the creek, the smell of moss, leaves, and earth, and peace.

When he awakened, he checked the minnow bucket, pulling it from the creek if there were enough, and leaving it if there weren't, but always he stayed as the sun rode the sky to its resting place. He listened for the hush, then for the first calls of the night birds which signaled it was time to go. Only then did he take up the minnow bucket, and earlier in his life, his gun, and walk back to the truck.

Today, he settles into the cradle of the roots and takes up his book, and as the sun strikes him through the diminishing canopy of the autumn oak, his head lolls back into the crease of the tree, the book spread-eagle on his belly, and he dreams.

Stand here with me and I will show you something different. I will show you how there is a grimace on his face that doesn't wake him, but it doesn't belong there either. Then I will show you the complete unnatural relaxation of his body, and I will tell you of his dream.

He dreams of old mountains without gates, of ginseng, of mushrooms, and the silver belly flash of trout, of quiet, watchful deer, and frolicking squirrels, of the path to the creek, of the oak. Then he hears a voice that *awakens* him.

"Hey, Don!"

Don raises his head and sees his old friend Gene striding toward him, and Don's heart leaps at seeing his friend. It has been a long time. Gene keeps a still further up the creek, deeper into the woods where the water is birthed from the mountains. There is no trail or path because Gene walks on the creek rocks, then braves the towering briar thickets to reach that secret place. No one knows where it is except Gene. He looks the same, maybe even a little younger – the crew cut with a bald center on his peaked head, the grayish stubbly beard, a stained wife-beater that is more tan than white stretches over his paunch, tan work pants, untied, cracked brown work boots, and a bandy-legged strut.

Gene is missing his front teeth on the top and bottom so when he laughs he looks like a jolly vampire. He is also a little crazy. He dislikes paying for anything he can get for free, and back in the day Don would loan Gene his boys to dig coal. Before the gates went up, Gene dug a mine in the side of the hill. It didn't have braces to keep the walls from caving in, and it was damp and cold. Gene had a little burro he used to haul the coal they dug out with shovels and picks, just as Don's grandfather had done. And the coal – it was perfect, soft, rich, bituminous, it was the finest coal you could mine. Yes, the dust clung to everything, but it burned long and hot, so hot the coal stove occasionally glowed orange. Lou yelled that he was going to set the house on fire as they sat fanning themselves, sweat beading on their upper lips. Don laughs at the memory and stands.

Then he realizes, Gene is dead, has been for almost twenty years. Suddenly, Don is afraid. He hears a whip-poor-will, but, that's a night bird. Wasn't it just morning?

"It's okay, Don. I brought someone with me."

Gene turns and behind him is Lou, a Lou from long ago. She's standing across the creek, and she's willowy and dark-headed, lush and young, just as he had seen her the first time.

"Don!" she calls and holds out her hand. The woods hush, and he walks away from his body to the night bird's song. It's time to go home.

Tom Thumb

You just never know when the shit coming around the corner is coming at you. You can try to outrun karma, but I gar-un-tee, she'll find you, just like she found that asshole Tom Thumb. Well, his name ain't Tom Thumb, it's Tom Adkins, and you'll know why we call him Tom Thumb here in a minute.

First, though, you have to meet my friend Eustace. Now, Eustace works at the Shop & Save unloading eighteen wheelers and stacking shit in the freezer. He's probably the only person I know who can do a wheelie on a forklift and not kill hisself. One day, though, he was walking through the warehouse and a box fell off the top shelf. Eustace put his hands up to protect his head and the damn box caught on his thumb and pert near ripped it off. He had to go up to the big hospital and have a little Asian doc sew all the ligaments and tendons back where they belonged. Then they had to do it again for some or another reason, and then Eustace had to go to the physical therapy place. This took a lot of time.

Time ain't something that Tom Adkins likes real well. See, he couldn't fire Eustace because Eustace was in the union and on the Workers' Comp. In those days it was before they had all the rules about who can talk to your doctor. About two years in, ole Tom thinks it's his place to go up to the big hospital and have a talk with Eustace's little Asian doc. According to what the little Asian doc told Eustace, Tom had asked him if it just wasn't easier to cut Eustace's thumb off than go through all rigmarole of putting it back together right.

Apparently the little Asian doc told Tom the Asian equivalent of "Get the fuck outta here!" I'd have like to seen that. Tom don't give up easy though because it wasn't the only time he had a chat with Eustace's little Asian doc, and it wasn't the only time the little Asian doc sent Tom packing.

Tom's a dick anyway, and he likes to wave his around, as in, can't keep it in his pants. He was round about on this third marriage to a lady from up the river named Cheryl. Must be the name because every chick I know named Cheryl is flat fucking nuts. Despite her being nuts, I mean kill-you-in-your-sleep-by-leaving-an-unlit-stove-on-crazy, Tom was out waving his dick around and word got back to Cheryl. She didn't wait until he was asleep, though. She broke a bottle of Boone's Farm over his head and stabbed him with the jagged neck. You'd think she'd try for something vital, like his heart, if he has one, or the jugular. Nope, either that or she missed and ended up pert near cutting his thumb off. That's right, y'all, his thumb! Now you know why we call him Tom Thumb.

And you'll never guess who was on call that evening at the big hospital. I bet you did guess. Yep, Eustace's little Asian doc. I didn't know they had hollers in Asia, but Eustace's little Asian doc must have come from one because Connie Light, who was over at the big hospital with her mom, was peeking through the curtain and said he rolled his doc chair up to Tom's bed and asked if it just wouldn't be better to cut it all the way off rather than going to the trouble of putting it back together right. Tom's face turned bright red and he called the little Asian doc a "gook" and "slant eyes" and a few other choices words and told the little Asian doc they should have killed him and his family in Vietnam when they had the chance, to which the little Asian doc answered, "I'm Korean."

"Well, they should have skunked your asses in Korea then!"

"We were on your side."

I'm not so sure I would be insulting the man who was going to make the decision as to whether I got to keep my thumb or not, but as you can tell Tom ain't the brightest bulb in the bug zapper. Regardless of how Tom treated him and treated Eustace, the little Korean doc sewed Tom's thumb back on. I'd like to say he sewed it on backwards or something like that, but he sewed it on straight, and Tom acted like ain't nobody ever had a finger cut off before. What a sissy. He walked around with it all bundled up and cradled against his chest and looked at everybody who came close to

43

him like they was going to try to cut it off again. He said he was traumatized. Whatever.

Eustace was sick of Tom's bullshit so he planned a little surprise for Tom. It seems that Tom, who's this big hulking guy, liked to run up on Eustace's backside while they were clocking out. He liked to hover over Eustace because Eustace ain't that tall. Here in the holler we call that "Little Dick Syndrome." It goes along with the guys who drive those souped-up trucks with the big tires and mud flaps who rev their engines behind you at the one stop light in town and pass you on the double yellow lines like they got the diarrhea shit-shits. I normally hang my head out the window and yell, "Sorry for your little dick!" You know you've done it.

Anywho, Eustace went over to his mama's for five straight days and ate her pork and pintos. They ain't nobody makes pork and pintos like Miss Ellen, and I gar-un-tee, you'll not forget you've had 'em. Lawd! The farts are unforgettable. You know it's bad when you fart and run away from yourself, even worse, those pork and pinto farts are clingers. You have to work to get those farts to go away. And as if the smell ain't bad enough, bad enough they make your eyes water, bad enough it makes dogs howl, getting those farts out is like shitting a lit match. Feel the burn, baby! They're so good going down, yet so lethal coming out. Well, you can imagine when Eustace told us he bottled all that up for five days, not only were we impressed but also surprised he was still alive. I was shocked he didn't spontaneously combust!

Eustace wears an insulated freezer suit, which is a fancy name for a snowsuit minus the little hand mittens. Of course, the only outlet for hot air is around the neck opening. After five straight days of pork and pintos and holding his asshole shut, Eustace waited until Tom slid up on his backside and let it go. Eustace said it felt like an M80 coming out of his ass. One of his coworkers said he saw a green cloud come out of that freezer suit so he made a run for it. Eustace said one second Tom was laughing, which is really a little piggy snort, and the next second he was gagging and then he vomited all over himself and passed out.

When Tom passed out he fell on his hand and broke it, plus he had a pretty bad concussion from hitting the concrete with his inflated ego. Several of the workers got sick and were off work for a few days, the little Shop & Save had to fumigate the dock area and file paperwork for a toxic leak with OSHA, although they never could figure out where that toxic leak came from. Eustace was off work too, although it wasn't for the same reason as everybody else. The Shop & Save has a really stupid policy of making anyone coming back to work after being off on Workers' Comp take a week of vacation. No lie. On Eustace's first day of vacation, he cut the end of his finger off in a band saw.

Seriously folks, you can't make this shit up.

Hardscrabble Road

The Big Dipper hangs between the mountains as though it had been born there, its handle like a thread from the center of a spider web reaching for the tips of the skeletal tree branches but never quite touching. Angeline loves the way the hollow opens up and frames the sky. Even in the deepest heat of summer there is always a breath of winter from the head. She sits on the steps of her trailer, the wood cold beneath her, her breath shows in the pale light of the half-moon that glows on the edges of the trailers. The chrome grill guard on her husband's truck sits in shadow, and it reminds her of an angry beast, just like him.

Dale is asleep in the little trailer, passed out drunk in the ragged easy chair, the anemic light from the television flickers across his face, the day's stubble like coal dust on his cheeks and chin. Angeline traces the raced welt along her cheekbone, then drops her hand, remembering how her mother always told her not to worry bruises and scrapes or they would never heal. She lights another cigarette, as though drawing the pungent, hot smoke into her lungs will warm her. She shivers, then she hears it - the train.

Even a mile and a half from the crossing, hidden in the snaking deep hollow, the whistle always finds her. Two short warning blasts, then a long echoing cry as it blows through the crossing, which didn't make sense because if you were already in the crossing blowing the whistle wasn't going to save your life, and everybody knew that. Right now the bells are tolling, red lights are flashing, and the gates are lowering, the ones so many ignore, anxious to cross the tracks, then the river, before they are stuck.

Angeline sways as she imagines the train, its steel grooved wheels singing, the rails sinking and rising in a mesmerizing rhythm as the cars carry away the coal that appears powdery as it blows away in a fine mist, but it isn't. It's sticky, like soot, and it clings to houses, the dead weeds and rocks, and in the summertime the leaves on low hanging branches will be black, black likes the lungs of miners and the slurry ponds that dot the pitted landscape, which is disappearing as fast as dynamite can eat away the mountains.

The clear night is bitter, and Angeline squeezes herself tighter, causing the rising knots on her shoulder and hip to ache. Dale had thrown her against the cabinet and smacked her until his hands and her face were stinging and red, then he had punched her. Angeline had cowered as he kicked her, screamed as he wound her hair around his fist, and drug her to her feet.

"Why can't you have my goddamn dinner ready!"

But that was it, you see. Dale works as a mechanic at King's, which had been bought out, but everyone still called it King's, and sometimes they were busy and sometimes they were slow. Angeline never knows when he will be home. Sometimes it's around four, like today, when she's unprepared, sometimes six or seven, and sometimes Dale doesn't come home until one or two if he decides to stop by the beer joint. He never calls. She never knows. It is a malicious game he plays with her every day.

He had followed her around the kitchen, barking at the back of her neck.

"Are you fucking stupid? You been lazin' around all day? This fucking place is a goddamn pig sty!" He had scraped his finger along the countertop and held it up to her face, dirty oil ground into his fingerprints, but nothing else.

"No wonder your Mama left you, you're a goddamn idiot!"

She had. There was no denying that, and Dale loves to rub it in, that, and her daddy sitting in the state penitentiary for murder. He'd strangled his girlfriend, Jody, to death not twenty feet from where Angeline sits, and then dumped her body down by the turnhole.

She was seven when Jack Vealey rode back into her life on a coughing, guttural motorcycle. He was a tall, lean man with a dusty red beard, his arms like cords of hewn logs.

He had high cheekbones and pock marks from the acne that had ravaged his teenage face, but he also had an energy, a magnetic energy that drew people to him, especially her mother, Josie. He was charismatic, defiant, and violent. One moment he was whispering in Josie's ear, her eyes captivated until they slid closed and she followed him into their bedroom and shut the door for the afternoon. The next moment he was slamming that same door, cussing, throwing things, or throwing Josie. Angeline slid under her bed, forcing her head between the rail and the floor, and stopped breathing to listen. There was something dark inside of Jack. Angeline could hear it in his voice, his second voice, the whisper voice, the voice that hissed, deeper than anger, a black twisted rage coiled inside of him. She never knew if anyone else could hear it.

One day, Jack told Josie to go fuck herself, bought the trailer, and moved it up Hardscrabble Road, less than half a mile from Angeline. It seemed like only a few days later that he came and got her, and never brought her back. He hadn't answered her questions about her mother, so Angeline walked to the trailer park. It was in the dead heat of summer when the creek was a mere trickle, only the deepest holes still held tiny swarms of minnows, and crawdads scuttled backwards under mossy rocks. There were no cicadas that year, but plenty of dusty green grasshoppers that popped like heated corn along the roadside. Grooved tracks in the sour mud were all that was left as her mother's trailer had been pulled out, leaving an empty space.

Another trailer was moved in, a tooth in the grinding gears of poverty is easily replaced, the space filled, but it looked odd to Angeline as she rode by on the school bus, like a new tooth among older teeth, glowing whiter and healthier than the others clustered around it. The space within her remained empty, empty like the mailbox, and empty as the silence of the phone that never rang.

Her father brought home strange women to play mother to her, or not, and most looked like Josie, or had a name like Josie, but Jody was the first, and only, who was strung out so hard. That was Jody's bad luck. She was a tiny thing with bad teeth, meth mouth, and Angeline had not known how old she was because all meth heads look ancient. Angeline had first seen her, or rather, her scabby arm, as Jody stood tweaking with the refrigerator door open.

Sometimes she was awake for days. Sometimes Angeline found her sprawled on the floor. Maybe she had stooped to pick something up, forgotten, and just laid down and passed out, or maybe she had crashed mid-stride and crumpled. Sometimes she made it to the chair, her legs slung over the arm, her hand limp on the floor, drool stretching from her open mouth, pooling into a dark spot on her light blue shirt. Jody died in the shirt. It may have been the only one she owned.

Angeline discovered being a meth head involved a lot of running for drugs. It seemed the trailer door slammed repeatedly, all hours, as Jody sought drugs and people brought drugs. One morning, Angeline came out of her bedroom and started down the hallway toward the kitchen when she heard her dad and Josie talking, or rather, Josie begging for her junk and what she was willing to do to get it.

"I suck you off, I suck you off, I suck you off, come on come on, Jackie, honey. Whadyawant? Whadyawant?"

Angeline darted back in her room and shut the door, waited for the two of them to walk by to their bedroom, right beside of hers, then took her book bag and left for school two hours early. That was the way it was – Jody high, Jody tweaking, Jody begging, doors slamming, Jack beating Jody, Jody crashing, Jody high, high, high, and tweaking and begging, and Jack's temper exploding. Then another woman named Teresa started coming by and the noises from the bedroom took a different turn. This is when Angeline learned to sneak out of her window. She didn't go far. She was afraid someone would tell Jack they had seen her out roaming, but it was better than sitting and listening.

Jack tired of women like eating the same thing every day makes you sick of it, but Jody seemed to stick, or maybe it was the game and the control. That's what Jack liked, the control, the manipulation, and Jody's near constant seeking put her in the position to satisfy his every whim.

One day, maybe two months into it, Angeline came home from school and when she stepped into her room she felt as though everything had been carefully picked through. Angeline didn't have much, but what she did have, she guarded. Maybe the corner of a book was askew where before it had been straight, or a drawer wasn't quite as flush as before, or maybe Jody had just left her funky, scabby energy behind, but whatever it was, Angeline read it. She jerked the bottom of her jewelry box out, and it was no surprise that it was empty. She was smarter than that, but when she pulled the drawer all the way out, the small piece of tissue that contained her grandmother's earrings was gone.

The earrings were small silver filigree hearts with a minute diamond chip in the center. When her Nana had died, her cousin Jessie made sure the earrings were passed to Angeline. It was the only thing Angeline had left of her mother and the family she was no longer allowed to see.

Angeline strode through the trailer, the floor wobbling and creaking with force of her steps. Jody was watching a game show and bouncing up and down on the edge of the couch. Angeline caught her on the up-bounce and pushed her. Jody staggered but caught herself on the arm of the couch. Before she could speak, Angeline slapped her.

"Where are my earrings, bitch? Huh? You trade 'em for some dope?" *Slap.* "You whore!" *Slap.* "Huh? Where the fuck are my earrings?" *Slap slap.* Jody cowered and Angline grabbed her hair, jerked her up, and punched her, a neat, quick jab that snapped Jody's head back and bloodied her nose. She sat down on her ass, and Angeline kicked her in the face, straddled her body, and balled her fists. Every time she tried to answer, Angeline punched her. It was unfair and traitorous, but the power she wielded at that moment in her powerless life she enjoyed. It scared her. It shamed her. But it didn't stop her until her Uncle Mike came in and asked what was going

50

on. Angeline jumped up, kicked Jody once more, and told him about the missing earrings.

"Do you know where she took them?"

Mike said he had an idea and told her to get in the truck. Mike's Rottweiler, Duke, hung out the window whining as Angeline approached.

"Shut up, Duke," she said, and he hushed, his docked tail vibrating as she jerked the door open. The truck reeked of marijuana and wet dog. The seat was covered with muddy paw prints. Duke licked Angeline's face, her hair, and the elbow she threw up to guard against his loving assault. Her hands shook, the very tops of her knuckles bruised and swollen.

Mike was a huge man. He topped off his massive girth with a floppy camouflage hat that hid the bald spot on the back of his head, pulled low to his eyebrows so all you saw was his bushy red beard and a broad nose with a knob on the end. He drove hunched over the wheel so his head didn't hit the top of the cab. Duke settled on his haunches and leaned against Angeline as the truck bounced over the ruts on Hardscrabble Road before Mike turned them toward Camp Two. Mike pulled truck off the road in front of a dilapidated single wide with a sagging, rotten porch.

"Just stay here," Mike said, and pushed the door open with his foot, "Earrings, huh?"

"Yeah, little silver hearts with a diamond in the middle."

Duke laid down with his head on Angeline's lap. A few minutes later, Mike came out.

"Here."

Angeline held her hand out and Mike put the earrings in her palm.

"I'd put them in your ears and keep them there."

When Jack came in that evening and asked what happened, Angeline answered.

"I fucked her up for stealing my earrings to get her junk," and continued eating her dinner, a bowl of generic

51

cereal that had gone stale. She raised her eyes just in time to
see a look pass from Jack to Jody. It wasn't a look of
recrimination or anger, but a fleeting look of fear, and Jody's
silent acquiesce. It was then Angeline knew it wasn't Jody
who had stolen the earrings.

Nothing much happened for the next week, other than
the money dried up, and Jody was tweaking and heading
toward the crash and had been that way the better part of two
days when Angeline heard a truck door slam over the whir of
the box fan. A few seconds later she heard the screen door
slam and saw the top of Jack's head go by and Mike's voice.

Angeline turned the knob on the top of the fan and the
motor stilled and the blades chopped the air until they too
were silent.

"Whadya mean?"

"You said she was crashin'. She'll be ready for the
junk. I got seventeen guys gonna be here by 7:30. Two
hundred apiece, and a few of 'em said they'd pay extra for a
go on her afterward. Don't fuck this up for us, Jack. I can see
it in ya, ya big sissy. Get the money and get rid of her before
she blows it all. Buy your daughter some fucking school
clothes, ya dumb fuck."

Only Mike could get by with talking to Jack like that,
and Jack didn't need to know he was charging three hundred.
He'd paid fifty bucks to get the earrings back and although he
could afford it, it didn't bother him to screw his brother out of
the money and then some.

"I brought that old window air conditioner and some
chairs. We can get this place moved around and I'll go pick up
Duke and the junk. I told Marge to give Duke a bath. Here,"
Angeline heard the jingle of metal on metal, "Go dress your
bitch up. Do it."

Angeline leaned against the wall as Jack came by,
sweat breaking out along her forehead. She turned the fan on,
low this time, and sat in front of it. She heard the screen door
again, and Jack's voice, their bedroom door shutting, and
Angeline crab-walked to her closet where there was a fist-

52

sized hole, really where Jack's boot had broken through in one of his rages. Angeline had a piece of black t-shirt stuck in the hole, but she winnowed out a corner and it was as though she was in the room with them.

Jack told Jody he found her some junk and some of Mike's friends were going to come by and all she had to do was be nice to them and maybe play around with the dog a little, wear the collar, make it look good.

"Whadya mean, Jackie? That's for fuckin' dogs."

"That's what you're gonna be doin' bitch, fuckin' dogs. You don't like it, huh? You wanna die instead, 'cause I'll kill ya, I'll strangle the life right out of ya. How 'bout this, how 'bout this," and Angeline hears a click, "I just blow those rotten teeth out of your head along with your brains? Open your mouth, open your mouth!" Angeline pressed her eye against the hole and saw Jack with his hand around Jody's neck, the other hand held his .22, and he pressed the barrel against Jody's mouth, and she pushed against him and shook her head, "Huh? No? Then shut the fuck up and do as you're told."

Angeline felt nauseous, the sweat pouring off of her, and she crawled out of the closet and turned the fan on high, the screen door opening and slamming, and opening and slamming.

"Angeline!"

Fuck. Jack blocked the hallway.

"Go down the road for a while, a couple of hours or so."

"Bullshit," Mike said, "Hey, Ang, you can go over to my place and keep Marge company."

She rode with Mike to his double-wide with air conditioning and cable TV, and she and Marge watched *Hee-Haw* and *The Beverly Hillbillies* re-runs on some oldies channel. Marge has a slight lisp and fire red hair. She made Angeline grilled cheese sandwiches and opened a can of real Campbell's Tomato Soup, and even though she had to put on already worn clothes, she let Angeline take a shower. It was a

53

small blessing for Angeline to step out of the foggy bathroom into comfort and coolness, her skin free of salt. But as Marge cackled at *I Love Lucy*, Angeline was thinking of Jody and the earrings and Duke, and how much she wished she could scrub her dad's words from her memory.

When Angeline left for school that fateful morning, Jody had been puttering around the kitchen to the smell of coffee and burnt toast. It bothered her that she couldn't remember if either of them had said good-bye.

Angeline didn't go to the funeral. She was sitting at a group home waiting on someone to claim her. Her cousin, Jessie, tried, but the social worker didn't want Angeline to change schools. She felt it was best to keep Angeline's life as close to normal as possible. In reality, the social worker was getting a kickback from her foster parents to place more kids with them. Instead of going to Jessie's comfortable two-story house, Angeline went to live in a doublewide that had been modified so many times it looked like one of those crazy, anti-government compounds on the six o'clock news. Her roommate was a sixteen-year-old who cut herself.

When she turned eighteen she married Dale and moved back, hoping to sell the trailer and start over, but no one wanted to buy a place where violence and death had visited. They had nowhere else to go, so they stayed right there on Hardscrabble Road, deep in the hollow where the creek scours the rocks smooth, and sometimes, during spring, it rises with the rain, and you can hear it rushing, rushing, rushing.

She used to dream the creek flooded the entire hollow, it had before, and she had been adrift in the muddy water, only the rooftops of houses visible as she flashed by with the empty milk jugs, deadfall, plastic, and scraps of clothing to become tangled in the branches of the trees, the fetid water creeping up their trunks. Then the water would recede, and she was left with all the other dead, alone.

Angeline's fingers, ears, and nose are numb, and her cheeks are starting to hurt from the cold despite the hot tears running down them. She's been tasting salt for a while now, but she's afraid to go inside, afraid he'll wake up when the handle rattles on the screen door, when the hinge squeaks, when the edge of the door held together with duct tape runs over the new plush doormat which is so out of place where it meets the stained carpet that has lost its pile. She's afraid to wake him, afraid he'll want to have sex, which he normally does, and it's the worst, the worst of it all. Not just that he mocks her body, her little tits, her fat ass, neither of which are true, but the pain, the pain of him penetrating her in her fear, the dry vessel which no longer welcomes him, and the way he stays inside of her after his orgasm, she's never had one, and tells her he has to so they'll make a baby, breathing in her face, sour and smoky, and she prays, Lord she prays the IUD holds tight.

I want to die, she thinks, and somewhere a voice in the wind, in her mind, says no.

"Yes, I do," she whispers, and she stands up and stumbles forward. She thinks at first it's the blood rushing back from where she's been sitting cramped up, then realizes the cold has seeped into her toes, her feet, but walking will cure that. Her shoes are thin and flat, not made for the cold, much less walking. She steps over the frozen puddles on the low water bridge, then onto the dirt driveway where apexes of gravel pieces push up into her feet.

She used to think she was tough, that she could handle anything, but those gravel pieces proved her wrong. They always found a way, whether she was barefoot or in flip-flops or tennis shoes, to bruise her heels or scrape her toes, but not tonight. She zips her jacket all the way, then flips the hood up. Wisps of blonde hair tug free and ride like fairies on the dull black fabric.

Christmas lights are wound around the chain-link fence next to the road. They are out, but the bulbs still glint in the moonlight. It is well past Christmas, but the Harpers are old and never take the lights down. Fake icicles hang with real ones along the edge of their roof. It is friendly and warm during the holidays. Angeline wishes one of the Harpers would have thought to turn the lights on tonight. She wants to see them one more time.

Icy puddles crack under her weight as she winds her way through the hollow. The Simpson's dog hears her light steps, its chain rattling first from within the dog house, then over the frozen earth as it snuffs and howls as she passes by. It's a boxer-pit mix, brindle with a white star on its chest. Sometimes Corey Simpson walks the dog and it lets Angeline pet its face and rub its ears, but it didn't like for you to walk by or come onto their property. The dog is almost bigger than Corey, but the dog adores the little boy, and Angeline wishes at least one of them was hers, in a different place, in a different time.

There is a trailer park at the mouth of the hollow. Angeline tucks her chin in her jacket and doesn't look at it. She never wants to see that trailer park again, not even now, not even to say good-bye. Instead, she flips it the middle finger and walks on, her heart full of the dark memories that reside there. But the darkest of memories are the ones that follow you, won't leave you alone, and they follow Angeline and beg for remembrance, even as her feet freeze and it becomes painful to walk on the road, but she slips and slides if she walks on the shoulder, so she weaves like a drunk, back and forth between now and then.

Angeline sucks tears in through her chattering teeth, rubbing them between chapped, numb lips, and looks to the other side of the road at the large brick houses that sit in the bottomland. She has never lived in a real house, one with a foundation, one that isn't moveable, that isn't made of tin and insulation, one that doesn't glow hot in the summer, and run cold in the winter.

One time, she and all of her classmates had been invited to a birthday party for Summer Dunfee. It was in the waning days of third grade in a time when you invited everyone to your parties. Mrs. Dunfee had set up a long table with a white plastic cover, balloons taped to the edges, and in the center was Summer's cake with nine candles and "Happy Birthday Summer" written in pink cursive icing. Angeline had never had a birthday party or a cake, not that she could remember. After three popsicles, Kool-Aid, and running in the early summer heat, Angeline had to pee, and asked Mrs. Dunfee on prancing toes where the bathroom was. Mrs. Dunfee had turned Angeline and pointed her up the steps of the brick house and told her to go in the front door and down the hallway.

Angeline had vaulted up the steps, pushed on the ornate black button on the heavy screen door, and pulled it open. Cool air flowed over her as she stood in the doorway, an unnatural silence within, no whir of fans pushing hot air around. The carpet was thick and maroon, all of the furniture matched, which matched the carpet, which matched the flowers and brass decorations on the walls. Angeline had looked down at her dirty toes hanging over the edges of her too small flip-flops, the smear of grass winding around her calf where she had slid outside, her raggedy shorts, and she tugged her t-shirt down, but it barely covered her belly. She was afraid to go into the clean brick house, afraid she would make it dirty and poor.

Instead, Angeline had run down the steps and around the house, and then squatted inside the crawl space to relieve her bladder, ashamed. There had been no time to retrieve her gift, which she believed was all wrong and not really a gift. She and Summer had won the three-legged race at field day, but Summer had gotten sick and had to leave, and Angeline had taken their ribbon home. She wanted to share it with Summer, and Angeline imaged they would trade the ribbon back and forth since they had won it together. Her stomach had tossed and turned as Summer broke open her homemade card and took the ribbon out. There was a look of surprise and genuine joy on Summer's face as she turned to Angeline and thanked her. Summer had moved in the middle of fourth grade, and Angeline hadn't seen her or the ribbon since. She wishes she had gone into the clean brick house. She wishes Summer had given her the ribbon back. It was the only thing she had ever won.

The moon has moved and it reflects off the thin layer of ice on the stagnate runoff from the rain and snow. A shallow pool of water sits in that depression. It never dries up. In summer, it stinks of decay, and even in the moonlight it is ugly, muddy, and dead. Brambles tangle together, holding tight with their icy thorns, impenetrable even in winter, and deep in the distance, Angeline hears the train whistle, two short warning blasts, then a long, echoing cry as it blows through a crossing, probably the one at Lower Falls, close, but not too close.

She forces her feet forward, increasing her pace, gritting her teeth as pain knifes from her feet into her calves. The crossing comes into sight. The bell is silent, the lights are dead, they have not yet begun to sing. A thousand feet up the river from the crossing, the train will hit the apex of the grade and make a wide sweeping curve as the grade declines toward the river bottom. It always picks up speed there. Down river from the crossing it disappears into another curve and a stand of poplar before following the river for another twenty miles. It is dark in those trees. The shadows will hide her until that last moment, and the engineer will never have enough time to stop, not with tons of steel and coal up his ass.

Angeline doesn't go to the crossing. She steps onto the white gravel that lines the rails and winces. Goddamn gravel, always digging into her feet. She squats beside the rail and puts her hand on it. It is frigid, even in her cold hands. It isn't singing. She looks upriver and holds her breath as the wind whips out of the hollow, bringing with it the sound of chugging. Yes, it is getting ready to top the grade, then she will see the light, and the rails will start to sing.

Trooper Manuel Stravrakis guides his SUV with his wrist slung over the steering wheel. His eyes are grainy, and he glances again at the digital clock on the dashboard. By the time he makes it back to the detachment, it will be time to go home. His right hand throbs from a scuffle during an arrest the day before. It is fucking cold, and he is tired. He passes by Hardscrabble Road, and like Angeline, turns his head away from the trailer park. It is a cesspool of meth heads, pill heads, and domestic violence, and like her, it's where he started. In his youth, it had been a quiet community of struggling families. As mines opened and closed, the families had become more desperate, not realizing there was another world away from the hollow.

As he rounds the last curve, the red warning lights flash, and the bell begins tolling. Manny thinks of running through before the gates come down, but his honor gets the best of him. He stops, throwing the SUV into park. Manny sees her from the corner of his eye. He never would have seen her, never known she was there had she not turned as the train's light fell over her. Angeline Vealey. Angeline Dotson, he corrects himself. What the fuck? What the hell is she doing? Manny shakes his head and watches as she stumbles along the rails toward the trees. She steps in between the rails. Adrenaline surges through him. Her back is to the train, she doesn't cross, she keeps walking between the rails. Manny fumbles with his seat belt and throws his door open.

"Angie!"

She pauses and turns, the light hitting her full on, her features a mask, sallow, hollow, and she bows her head and begins walking again. Oh shit. Manny starts running.

They lived next door to each other. Manny first met her by the creek. She was turning over rocks looking for crawdads. Her hair hung down her back, and she tossed it, tendrils clinging to her sweaty cheeks, her skin dark, which Manny thought was strange. It made her sun-bleached hair more blonde, her eyes greener, and he noticed she only burned across the bridge of her nose. His family is Greek, and he was always darker than her. They used to compare their tans by holding their arms up side by side.

It wasn't long after Manny moved in that Jack came back. He remembered the day she had walked down Hardscrabble Road to the trailer park. She stood and cried in the empty trailer spot until his mother had gone outside and taken the little girl in her arms.

"That's Jack Vealey's girl," their neighbor offered, blowing cigarette smoke out as she talked, "He won't want ya coddlin' 'er." Angeline had long tear marks tracked through the dust on her face. Manny's mother got her keys, and at the last moment, Manny jumped into the car with them. He and Angeline sat together on the long bench seat as the car wound up the hollow.

Jack Vealey came out of the trailer scratching his bare belly. A skinny, sandy-haired woman with a black eye leaned on the door frame with her arms crossed. The tan trailer leaned with her, and they reminded Manny of slender, writhing copperheads, waiting with their forked tongues to devour his friend.

"I want my mommy," Angeline said as Jack jerked her out of the car.

"Shut up! Barb, get over here and get her," he said, and shoved Angeline toward the woman, "You were supposed to be watchin' her."

Barb stomped down the steps of the trailer and grabbed Angeline's hand.

"She said she was goin' to play. Stop your bawlin', child!"

When she stumbled, Barb picked her up by her wrist, her arm grotesquely elongated; her sobbing intensified and carried across the yard. Manny clenched his fists and almost started to cry himself. Jack leaned over and looked in the car.

"What are you waitin' for? A fucking reward?"

His mother cursed in Greek all the way home, and as soon as she stopped the car, Manny jumped out. He ran to the creek, hopping and jumping upstream, and knelt in the shadows, waiting, but she didn't come out of the trailer, not for a few days. When she did, she had bruises on her face, arms, and legs like half-moons, and when Manny asked her about them, she shrugged and told him her daddy whipped her with a belt for going to the trailer park. He was just nine years old, but he held her hand as they sat with their feet in the creek. He held her hand on the bus the first day of school too. Angeline hung to the back of the cluster of kids at the bus stop, her pants too short, her t-shirt too tight, her toes cramped in her shoes, and as he sat beside her, he could see a bruised knot behind her ear.

But that wasn't the worst of it. When Angeline was eleven and Manny thirteen, they had been out at the creek, hidden among the rocks and overhanging trees, not flipping stones and looking for crawdads, but talking. He had never kissed a girl before, but he knew he wanted to kiss her, so he did. When she looped her arms around his neck and kissed him back, he knew for sure what a hard-on was. It was awkward and chaste, and when they broke apart Angeline's eyes were wide, and they were both breathing too fast. Then, they heard Jack calling for her. Angeline popped up from the brush like a flushed quail and sprinted over the rocks. Manny followed her, hidden in the shadows. Jack flew down the steps and grabbed her arm.

"You been with that nigger!"

Manny flushed as anger boiled up. Angeline pulled back, but Jack held tight.

"He ain't a nigger! He's Greek, and if you wasn't such a goddamn idiot, you'd know the difference!"

Jack backhanded her. Angeline twisted and went down so fast she couldn't break her fall. She looked up as though she was choking, her lip split, hands cut and bleeding, the breath knocked out of her. Jack kicked her over with his foot, bent down, grabbed her face in his hand, and pulled her off the ground as though she were a puppet.

"Nigger! Sand nigger! Still a goddamn nigger! You

stay away from that little nigger, girl, or I'll kill ya, you and him!"

Jack dropped her back on the gravel and stood, his bare belly glowing white and distended.

"You hear me, nigger boy! Stop sniffing around with your dick!"

Manny cried. He sat in the shadows and cried for her and for his own cowardice, for his still short stature and the weak muscles that couldn't beat the fuck out of Jack Vealey. Jack went back into the trailer and slammed the door, but Manny, feeling every ounce the pussy, stayed hidden until he saw Angeline sit up, then stand, and she didn't look back as she limped away and went around the trailer, out of his sight. He knew she was going to the woods, to the cove, where she could get lost and lick her wounds.

Before her, Manny never knew there were coves in the mountains. Instead of rolling ocean troughs and white foam, the little flat was a sea of clover and wildflowers. Around them the hill rose in a steep, horseshoe shape, a sanctuary of oak, birch, poplar, and mottled sycamore just beginning to spread their leaves. Briars reached out and scraped their legs, snagged their clothes, and nettle stung them the moment they looked away. Sneaky nettle. When he slapped at a mosquito, his hand came away smeared with blood and sweat. She pointed out ramps, may apple, and a striped maroon jack-in-the-pulpit, lifted her eyes and found cardinals, blue jays, and a giant red-headed woodpecker hammering at a dead tree, as though knocking at the door of the mountain, wanting to be let in.

"Stop," she said, and pointed, "It's a lady slipper." Manny thought the broad green leaf with fine delicate white edging looked more like a tongue than a slipper. He peeked over her shoulder as she scanned the ground.

"What?"

"There," and she pointed again. Manny hadn't seen anything until she reached forward, made a twisting motion with her fingers, and presented him with a mushroom, its cap black and wrinkled, the stem fat and cream colored.

"What is it?"

"It's a molly moojer, silly."

"A what?"

She had laughed at his ignorance.

"A molly moojer, a morel. It's a mushroom. You eat 'em, and," she had turned and lowered herself closer to the ground, "if you look just right, you'll find more." Manny squatted next to her and there were more, spread along a straight line from where she had found the first.

"Some ain't black. There's gray ones and yellow ones too," she educated him as they combed the mountainside, "They like oak and poplar groves and dead trees too, and where you find one, you'll always find another, that is, if you're not standing on 'em."

As though expecting them, she pulled a crumpled plastic bag from her pocket and began filling it. When he asked her how she knew so much about the woods, she straightened and looked up at the blue sky between the trees.

"My family, my mom's family, I mean. They used to come up here all the time, but I don't see them anymore."

Manny wanted to ask about her mom, but Angeline turned her head, shrugged, and bit her lip, so Manny never asked, and as he imagined her walking along the trail among the stinging nettle, he hadn't follow her. He went home.

That night he heard a tapping on the door and her soft voice, and his mother called for him. Angeline waited at the base of the steps for him, like she always did, as though she weren't good enough to stand on the porch or at the threshold. Manny closed the door behind him.

"I'm sorry for what he said."

"You need to go home, Angie."

"But. . ."

"He'll kill ya, and I won't be the cause of it. You just need to stay away from me."

"No!" Her mouth dropped open, and he could see tears at the edges of her wide, panicked eyes.

63

"I'm sorry." He turned and went back into the trailer as she stretched her hand out. He never knew how long she stood at the bottom of the steps and sobbed into her elbow, waiting for the door to open again, until finally she gave up and whispered. . .

"Oh, Manny."

Yes, she knows that voice, and she stops, her body quaking with cold and the resonance of it. In her mind's eye, she again watches him shut the door on her, her outstretched hand moist with tears and sweat, but empty of the strength he had given her to endure. She sat looking out the window of the school bus so as not to search him out as he sat with someone else, but sometimes she caught his eye across the lunchroom.

The last time she saw him was through the door of the trailer. He stood near the creek behind several police officers, and as the county sheriff led her father out in handcuffs, Manny had a small, cruel smile at the corners of his mouth. It scared her, the malice she saw in his eyes. It scared her how quiet her father was, how easy it was for them to bang on the trailer door and for Jack Vealey to allow them, *allow them* to handcuff him, and lead him away like a whipped dog. What passed between them, him and Manny, as Jack had been put into the cruiser? Hate? Vindication? Whatever it was, it had not helped her.

"Angie!"

Manny slides on the tall weeds, slick with frost. He isn't going to make it.

Hooty Milam has been an engineer with CSX for fifteen years. He knows the rails like the back of his hand, still, he doesn't notice the woman standing in the tracks, her pale face and blonde hair turned away from him. Her shadow melts into the darkness of the trees as he picks his spit can up, spits, and returns it, his attention turned at just the right moment to miss it all.

"Damn you, Manny," Angeline whispers, and she steps back, the air from the engine rushing over her, her nose inches from steel and aluminum, her feet resting at the edge of a tie that rises and falls with the rhythm of the train, the grooved wheels singing on the rails.

Manny reaches out, sinks his fingers into her jacket, and jerks her away from the train, throwing them both off balance. Angeline steadies herself, then strides forward on numb, stumbling feet and smacks him.

"Fuck you, Manny!"

Pain explodes in her frozen limb all the way to her shoulder, and she cries out. Manny grabs her by the jacket and shakes her.

"What the fuck are you doing!"

Angeline cradles her head in her hands and sobs as Manny pulls her into his arms and crushes her against him. At first, she doesn't know where she is. She believes she is frozen because she is unable to feel him, a softness, flesh, until she realizes it is his body armor that keeps them separated. Maybe it has always been her armor. She presses her face into his warm neck. Somehow she is inside the SUV, the gates are going up, and they are speeding away from the tracks, from the hollow, from Hardscrabble Road.

Manny pulls off in a wide spot half hidden in shadow. Angeline wipes at her face, smearing snot and tears like a child. There is a bandanna in the glove box, and Manny wipes her face with it and presses it into her hand.

"What the fuck, Angie! You scared the life out of me!"

She turns her head, the welt on her cheek visible in the glow of the dashboard. It reminds him of the knot behind her ear on the school bus. It reminds him of that day, the day he let her crawl away alone, of his cowardice, and the sick satisfaction of seeing Jack Vealey in handcuffs. It's what compelled him to apply to the State Police Academy on his

65

twenty-first birthday - to wear the olive drab uniform, the triangular shield, the flat-billed ranger hat, the badge.

Angeline doesn't answer him.

"I'm not takin' you home. I can see what Dale's done to ya."

"Should've left me alone. It didn't bother ya the last time."

"Well, I couldn't do anything the last time."

She condemns him in a glance. Manny puts the truck in gear and pulls out. He tells her about the women's shelter in the city, how they can give her a place to stay, some clothes, help her find a job, maybe she can go to school. Angeline shakes her head.

"I got family," I do, she thinks, I do have family, "Can you take me somewhere to call my cousin?"

"Who?"

"Jessie Mullins. Does it matter? I got a half a million of 'em"

"I think I know who you're talking about. Did her husband die in the mines?"

"Yeah, like a long time ago."

Manny nods, "She's dating one of the county deputies."

It's after eleven when they reach the low cinderblock building that serves as the local State Police detachment. The floors are marbled linoleum that hides stains, the walls are blinding white, and broken up by black-framed photographs of stern-faced officers. Manny lays a tattered phone book on the desk and tells her to dial "9" for an outside line. Angeline looks up Jessie's number, but hesitates before she picks up the receiver. She wonders if Manny can hear the buzzing dial tone from across the room. It's late, but she has nowhere else to go, so she dials, rehearsing in her mind what she will say. But when the female voice answers, she asks, simply,

"Jessie?"

"No, it's Flynn, hold on a sec. Wait, who is this?"

66

"It's Angeline."

There's silence on the other end, a crackle as the phone is covered, the muffled sound of Flynn yelling, a crackle as the phone is uncovered.

"Well, it's been forever," Flynn says, "Do you remember me?"

Angeline remembers her grandmother's strong hands on her shoulders, beans being strung into a dented, aluminum dishpan, someone braiding flowers in her hair, shiny black hair and startling silver blue eyes, a throaty laugh as minnows slip through their fingers. The memory triggers a longing that crushes her, a homesickness that transcends thought and memory.

"You used to braid my hair," Angeline says.

Angeline feels her smile through the phone. It's like sun breaking through clouds, a surge of love, longing, and remembrance.

"I did."

It's easy to forget, Angeline thinks, easy to forget the times she saw her family, although rare, they all live on this side of the county and beyond, but they remembered her. They hugged her, they pressed their phone numbers written on the edge of store lists into her hand and asked her to call, and she was too ashamed to tell them she didn't have a phone, and they asked her to stop by, don't be a stranger, y'all come now, and she was too ashamed to tell them she didn't drive. She hadn't invited them to see her because she wasn't allowed, *wasn't allowed*, like a child who isn't allowed a cookie before dinner. That's over, she thinks as she sets the phone in the cradle, that's over.

Jessie cries when she sees her, and hugs her as though she were her own child who was lost for so many years.

"You are as pretty as the sunrise," Jessie says.

"Always has been," Flynn says. But it's Flynn that Angeline can't stop looking at, she is stunning, and Manny is staring at her too, until Flynn turns and puts her hand out.

"Flynn Mullins."

"Manuel Stavrakis."

"Man-yule?"

"It's Greek," he says.

"I know," Flynn says, "But all this time I thought your name was Manny, Trooper Manny."

"It's a little easier. Stavrakis doesn't exactly roll off the tongue. You look familiar. Have we met before?" He knows better. He would not have forgotten.

"I work at the Courthouse. I'm Judge Starkey's law clerk. Maybe you've seen me in passing."

"Maybe."

"Well, we'd better get down the road. I 'preciate it, Manny," Jessie says.

Manny watches them walk out to the car and when Flynn looks back, he still can't believe she's Bill Mullins' granddaughter. Damn.

I Know What the Iblam Ladies Wear Under Their Habits

People think we're all white bread down here in the holler. Ain't so. Got a bunch of people descended from the Greeks and the Italians and the Poles that rolled up in here to work in the mines. They got funny names but they've been here a long time and nobody thinks much of it. It's the people named Mullins and Combs and Belcher that have the funny look about them. They ain't white bread. They ain't black neither. They's something else. Their whole families are messed up too, and I ought to know since I'm part Mullins.

I got three sisters and we're all different. I'm all dark-headed and dark-eyed and dark-skinned, and my next sister is blond-headed and blue-eyed and dark-skinned, and my next sister is blond-headed and blue-eyed and has skin so fair she burns if she thinks about the sun, and then there's Vicki. She's the redhead with brown eyes and so many freckles she looks like she has a tan. She's the meanest too. Racist to the core.

Now, I've said it before and I'll say it again, my mama's a little bit of a whore, so much so I often wondered if all of my sisters were my sisters, like full sisters. It wasn't until all of us were missing the same permanent tooth, the second one on the back bottom, two away from the fang tooth, just like my dad, that I was sure. You can imagine how the dentist felt coming out from the free clinic to tell my mama what he saw on the x-ray, about all of us not having a permanent tooth, and her saying, "Well, that proves it. They're all his."

Good grief.

Anywho, one day Vicki and I are wandering around town with the kids she was babysitting, Lucy Combs' twin boys, Elmer and Delmer, who I was convinced shared one brain cell, when we saw our first Muslims. They was walking down Main Street, kids in tow, looking just like that old Mother Superior from *The Sound of Music*. They just didn't have that white collar on that made them look like they had chicken neck. Vicki stopped dead and looked at me like it was my fault there were Muslims on the sidewalk.

"Are those goddamn Mooslims?"

Like I said, Vicki is racist to the core. She must of got most of mine because I say live and let live. I ain't got nothing against nobody who has to dress up like Mother Superior. It was so hot I had boob sweat, and I also had a fair bit of pity for the Muslim ladies having to come out all covered up. I'd learned in school about the Muslims and why they covered up, which Vicki probably needed a lesson in since her shirt that day pert near showed her nipples. She didn't have much to show, but, by golly, she was going to flaunt what she did have.

Elmer and Delmer were about two years old at the time, and you know how two year olds are, they pick up every little word you say and repeat it. While Vicki is going on and on about the goddamn "Mooslims," Elmer and Delmer start imitating her.

"Mooooo, mooooo." Oh hell. The Muslim ladies are walking toward us with Vicki still flapping her jaws and Elmer and Delmer going at it like it's a fucking barnyard. I jerked the stroller hard enough to give the boys whiplash.

"Shut up around the Islam ladies."

"Iblam, iblam, iblam, iblam," one of those two little twerps started and the other followed, that would never change, by the way, and the Muslim ladies walk by us and nod and I nod and Vicki pinches me in the arm, hard!

"Don't be nice to those goddamn Mooslims!"

"Mooooo, moooooo."

"Goddamn you, Vicki, that's gonna leave a bruise. I'd pinch your titty off if I could find it. They ain't nothing wrong with them any more than the Church of Godders not cutting their hair and wearing long skirts and shit, or the freaking nuns wearing their habits. Why shouldn't I be nice to them?"

"They're from I-ran or somewhere. Just fucking sand niggers."

I can't tell you how many times I've been called that. I don't know what's in my blood, but I don't look much different than them, and if I get a good tan on, I'm even darker, and don't think just because she's my sister that Vicki's never called me one. Plus, our sister Scarlet Ray, who everyone calls Sugar because she's the one with the white blonde hair, blue eyes, and white skin, is married to Max Anderson, who is a Rastafarian undertaker who wears these funky square-ish but cat-eye glasses that make him look like the love child of Bob Marley and Malcolm X.

I ain't gonna lie, my eyebrows shot straight up when she told us she was marrying him. Not that I don't like Max, I do, and not that I care that he's black, but, I guess, because people around here just don't do that very often, and we're strange enough as it is. He's funny as hell with that crazy accent, and he loves my sister. That's what matters most. He loves my sister to the moon and back. Vicki don't care how much he loves Sugar or how happy she is, or how cute their kids are, or how Sugar threatened her with bodily harm if she ever heard the n-word again. That don't stop Vicki.

"I'm really sick of that word, Victoria Bernice, and if I hear it come out of your mouth again, I'm gonna beat you to death."

I went to the family over it too. It's not the first time I've talked to the extended family about just ganging up on Vicki and putting our foot up her ass, but, for whatever reason, my momma just refuses to stand up to her, and if you can't get my momma to do it, the rest of the family ain't going to. Vicki causes a lot of trouble. I'm so sick of it.

About a year after that, and I know because I had boob sweat and boob sweat don't show up until about August, July in a bad year, when my cousin Thermy come busting up into the Rio D. I almost took her temperature. Somebody had to have died, otherwise my God-lovin', God-fearin', Church-of-Godder-to-the-ends-of-her-hair cousin would not be in a bar.

"Virgie!"

"Did somebody die?"

"No, it's even better! It's about the Mooslim ladies!" Thermy bellied up and wrestled herself onto a bar stool. She's a little on the hefty side, like her asshole was probably trying to swallow up the bar stool hefty.

"Well, while I'm here, I'm hungry. Would you fix me one of those cheeseburgers and some fries, and what's your pie today?"

"Pecan," I said, my eyebrows way up under my bangs, my mouth all gaped open like she just flashed me a tit.

"Oh, I'll have a piece of that too, and a pop, diet."

"Thermy, you're in a bar. Do you know that?"

"You serve food, it ain't no different than going to the Applebees and people sit around you drinking, and hurry up, I got to tell you about the Mooslims."

I slapped some burger on the grill, cut her a double-sized piece of pecan pie, and ran her a diet from the bar gun.

"Well, ain't that neat."

"Damn it, Thermy, will you just tell me about the Muslim ladies!"

"Okay," and she flashes me jazz hands, "you know I've been working over at the little pitcher place on Main, right?"

"Right."

"Well, one of them Mooslim ladies comes in and wants her pitcher taken, but without her hair scarf."

My eyebrows go up again.

"Really?"

"Yes, but I can't be there when she takes it off because she has to say some prayer thing and nobody's supposed to see her without it, but she wanted a pitcher for her husband. So I put her in the back room and give her a few minutes to let her do her prayer thingy and what have ya, and I walk in and. . ." Thermy covers her mouth like she's a seven year old who just said her first bad word, "She was butt nekkid from the waist down."

"Noooo."

"Yes she was! I didn't know what to do! I'm like, 'Lady, what are doing?' Then she tells me she only wants the pitcher from the waist up. I don't care! She can't be sitting there nekkid from the waist down on my pitcher stool. Good Christian people sit on that stool!"

I'm laughing so hard I can barely stand up, not just because the Muslim woman was naked, but because it was Thermy, and I doubted Thermy had been completely naked with her own husband, much less on a picture stool.

"I had to cover her myself! They're heathens, Virgie!"

"Well, it's hot! A woman's got to have some relief from the heat, especially if you have to walk around in a habit all day. Kind of makes you wonder about nuns, too, huh?"

"Virgie!"

I know, I know, I'm going to hell.

The Harbinger

You hear strange things in the mountains, that's for sure. I've heard stories of haints and boogermen and banshees that'll make you afraid to breathe out loud, let alone check under your bed. That's where horror movies get it wrong. I ain't never known anyone brave enough to look under their bed for whatever made a strange sound. I know I never did. I just laid there and hoped it went away, and here's why.

My Nana lived in a one bedroom apartment above the garage next to the big house. She'd been married to an ass her whole life and raised up sixteen children, fourteen of her own and two that she adopted. After the ass died, that would be my grandfather, Vic, she said the big house was too much to take care of herself, but she didn't want a bunch of bullshitters living with her either, so she moved to the apartment. My Momma said it was so none of the gadabouts could pawn their kids off on her permanent, except for Angeline. Angeline was always different. Nana just wanted some peace and quiet in her final years.

You had to climb a set of steep steps to get to the apartment. Nana said it kept her young, but they was so loud, she probably hid in the back if she didn't want company, and you'd never know she was there. But one night, right about nine, she was sitting in her favorite chair doing a crossword, she loved crosswords, and she heard someone a coming up those steps. Then she heard three knocks on the door.

She turned the outside light on and looked out the little peephole, but she didn't see anyone. Now, that landing ain't very big. You could see the whole thing through that peephole. She opened the door and looked, then stepped onto the landing and looked, she even craned her head around and looked up on the roof, but there wasn't anyone there. At least, not anyone you could see. Brave woman she was. Ain't no way I would have stepped out onto that little landing, much less looked on the roof. I guess she never saw that episode of

The Twilight Zone where that little gremlin thing is on the wing of the plane. Wing, roof, same thing to me.

Unlike me, my Nana didn't spook easy. Who do you think I heard about all of them haints, boogermen, and banshees from? She'd gotten married at fifteen and had the first of her fourteen youngens when she was sixteen. There wasn't much the woman hadn't seen herself or heard about from someone else. But she went straight inside and called my momma, who jerked me outta bed, and told me to stay awake while she was gone. My Aunt Sandy pulled into our driveway in her Cadillac. She loves Cadillacs like my Nana loved crosswords, and in those days they were as big as a boat and sounded like a jet taking off when she revved the engine. I think my Uncle Bart had something to do with that.

Momma wouldn't tell me what was going on, but I know she had time to call half my uncles before Sandy got there, and I suppose they all went and did a once over of the place to make sure Nana was safe. Well, it wasn't so much to make sure she was safe, Nana could take care of herself, but, you know, they wanted to know what was going on.

Anywho, the next night, right at nine, Nana heard the steps again and then the three knocks, and still, no one was there. She did call Momma again, but no one went this time. It was a knocking spirit. A harbinger of ill news, at least, that's what Great Aunt Bertie told Momma. Momma said she'd never heard of such a thing and that ill news is brought by the banshee, not some dumb ass knocking on the door.

Great Aunt Bertie pointed her cigarette at Momma and said, "The banshee is about death, Loretta, but the harbinger is about news, bad news." Momma pinched her face up, but she didn't argue. Bertie was just two steps below Nana in the family faith and if you pissed her off too much you might end up with in-grown toenails or a case of ass acne. Of all the elders, Aunt Bertie had some of the most imaginative forms of retribution. My sister Vicki sassed her one day and got cold sores all over her mouth and up her nose for a month. Too bad it didn't teach her anything.

Naturally, at least for our family, on the third night about half of the family shows up to wait. That means there's about ten of us younger grandkids piled up underneath the dining room table hoping to get the scoop on the harbinger by reading tarot cards. I don't remember exactly who all was there, but it was definitely my cousin Flynn, who was about twelve because she was just starting to get boobs, my sister Anna, who was about six and was sitting bowed up in Flynn's lap, probably my cousins, Angeline, because she stayed with Nana a lot, Russell, maybe Danny, hell, my sister, Sugar Ray, might have been there too, just crawling around and drooling on herself. Flynn had cut and shuffled the deck. She still has those cards, by the way, an old set of Nana's. Flynn pulled six cards and separated them into pairs.

"Let Anna do it," Flynn said. No doubt, we start 'em young. Now that I think about it, it's been so many years, I have no doubt Flynn already knew what those cards said. She was too cool, too prepared as she guided Anna's hand over the first two cards.

"What do you see?"

Anna leaned toward the cards and scrunched her face up. Flynn pulled her back.

"You're looking with the wrong eye. Relax." Anna sighed like a baby does before it falls asleep and settled her head against Flynn's shoulder. Then Flynn leaned forward and guided Anna's hand over the cards again.

"What do you see?"

Anna sighed again. Then her eyes shifted, like she was looking without seeing, but seeing something else.

"A baby, a baby boy!"

Flynn moved her hands to the next cards.

"What do you see?"

Anna turned her hand over and cupped it.

"Water."

Yeah, yeah, I'm sure Russell was there because it was Russell who spoke up. Like Anna, Russell has a gift for tarot, for "sight." I don't know if he saw what Anna saw or what Flynn had already seen, or if the cards tipped him off.

"Stop Flynn, she's too little."

"She has to learn," Flynn said and moved Anna's hand again, "What do you see?"

"Flynn, stop it!" He whisper-yelled it, because although Flynn may have stepped over an invisible line or breached a very gray area, Russell was also loyal to her. He wanted her to stop, but not enough to rouse the ire of the parents. Me, well, I was eight or nine and I remember The Sun card and a few Cups cards, and I definitely remember the next to last card. It was The Tower. A lot of people get all whipped out of shape when the Death card shows up in a reading. It's nothing, just change, transformation, and very rarely the type that goes from living to dead. But that Tower card, fuck, that's a whole other story - calamity, upheaval, the worst of the worst, a fate worse than death, a purgatory of pain.

A baby boy plus water plus a purgatory of pain. Jeezus H.

"What do you see?"

"It's hot!"

Anna tried to stand up and Flynn caught her just in time to keep her from banging her head on the bottom of the table.

"It's hot! It's hot!"

"Shhhhh, it isn't. You're fine, you're just feeling their feelings, you have to block that and just see."

"It's hoooooot!" Suddenly, there were twenty parent faces looking under the table. Flynn is rocking Anna and I can feel her energy working, but Anna let it get to her. She was too young to block it, and when Nana scooted her chair back and said, "Give her to me," Flynn let Anna crawl off of her lap. I can still see Nana's old white sweater, pilled and worn, a lump right at the wrist where she always kept a few tissues stashed.

"Get out here, Flynn!" her mom said, and Flynn crawled out among the legs, but when Jessie stood up, most

79

likely to take Flynn for an ass beating, Nana, who had already soothed and quieted Anna, said, "Leave her to me."

Those words scared me more than The Tower card. I'm not sure what Flynn's punishment was, she never has told me. Nana could be as harsh as she was loving, but with Flynn, the exalted and powerful Flynn, she leaned toward harshness.

About the time Flynn stood up to face Nana, the clock started chiming nine o'clock, and everyone hushed. Even from under the table, I could hear the footsteps on the stairs. It made the little hairs stand up on the back of my neck. As powerful as some people are in some ways, they can be equally ignorant in others. I honestly believe that only four people in the room had a clue what this was about – Anna, Russell, Flynn, and me. It's always interesting to see how the powers play out through the generations.

When Nana opened the door, all I could see were a pair of black shoes polished up like a mirror. It was Nana's cousin, Sheriff Hiram Belcher. He must have thought we were having a party because he apologized for the interruption. It seems my cousin Jenny had been calling the house phone but nobody would answer, and she needed Nana down at the hospital. She had gone to work and left her baby boy with a guy named Jarrod Chapman, one of her revolving boyfriends. Jarrod told the police that baby Wyatt was screaming and wouldn't stop so he tried to give him a bath to see if it would calm him down. The water must have been too hot though because he damn near scalded the skin right off of him.

Nana gathered up her herbs and went to the hospital and kept Wyatt for a few weeks after until he was fully healed. There was a lot of whispering during this time. I figure they were determining whether they were going to retaliate or not. Nana must have lost because she pouted for weeks. I heard my mother tell her to let karma run its course.

Three or four years later, Flynn came over to pick beans with me and Anna in the little garden behind our house. It was late August, the sun was blazing, and the flies were biting and the sweat bees were stinging, but we had to get it done because by noon it would be a hundred degrees and so humid it would be like breathing through wet dryer lint. I had just lifted a leaf on a mother-load of greasy grits when Flynn said,

"Hey, look! That house is on fire." Sure enough you could see black smoke billowing from across Frazier's Bottom.

It wasn't a few seconds more until we heard the volunteer fire department sirens. I wondered out loud who it was, and Anna answered, "Jarrod Chapman. There were two more, but they've already been taken." She had that faraway, seeing but not seeing look, and the way she said it made it sound like an alien abduction. I danced around trying to shake off the icky feeling. I still wonder why a big coward like me was allowed to be born into such a creepy family.

This was way before people started snorting Oxycontin and blowing up meth labs, but of course someone said Jarrod and them people had to been free-basing cocaine or someone dropped a Mary Jane roach. Actually, it was just a short in the cord on the box fan. True, both of Jarrod's buddies died from smoke inhalation, and Jarrod probably wished it had finished him off too. He had second and third degree burns all over the lower half of his body. My cousin, Thermy, said she heard at church that they had to put his boy bits on their own little pillow because they were so swollen. I was horrified to hear about his boy bits, and even more horrified that she had heard about it at church. I don't remember hearing such things in my three week stent as a Church of Godder.

Basically though, the heat from the fire cooked him from the waist down. It also cooked his insides, you know, from inhaling the heat. That's what really killed him, or caused him to die, I should say. Cooked flesh is swollen, tender flesh, and eventually his trachea couldn't support the breathing tube and it ripped a big hole in his throat and took out a couple of arteries. He sort of bled out and suffocated all at the same time.

I never did tell you that last tarot card from that ill-fated reading, did I? It was the Justice card. Karma takes her time, but she always gets her due.

The Haint

For every kind of beast, and of birds, and of serpents, and of things in the sea, is tamed, and hath been tamed of mankind: But the tongue can no man tame; it is an unruly evil, full of deadly poison. James 3:7,8

They say a haint is really just your conscience following you around, begging for attention. It's not what you think. Really, it's just your conscience.

That's what they say.

It started with a scratching in the wall of the Peeling Paint House. The Barker family turn their heads, their eyes searching for the source, the hot food before them unable to steam in the cloying humidity. The father, Hershel, looks away first, his eyes flicking from one family member to another, first passing over Ashley, the youngest, before settling his gaze on Muriel Jane.

She gnaws the edge of her lip, a small muscle flexing along her delicate jawbone. Feeling his eyes on her, she swivels her head to look at him, the corner of her mouth lifting in a sneer.

Darrell, the eldest, stops chewing, the food bulging in his jaw like a plug of tobacco. He sniffs, then starts chewing again. The scratching keeps time with him – a dry *sscccrrr* followed by a faint squeak.

With a thump, like a book falling from a shelf, the scratching stops. They flinch.

"What was it?" Ashley asks.

"It was a mouse," her mother Rose says. Hershel stares at her now, his elbows on the table, fingers threaded together. A louder thump, a book flying from the shelf, a screen door slamming in the wind, answers.

Ashley sinks down in her chair, dark eyes wide.

"That's not a mouse."

* * *

Muriel Jane, M.J. to everyone but her father, brushes her dark hair straight from a side part. She sets the brush on the bureau and brings her hands under her breasts, testing their weight. Perhaps they are a little fuller than yesterday.

All she had ever known about boys and sex were what she had seen in her brother's porn pile. She'd rifled through his collection, touching herself in the same places, fascinated by the sensations and the pictures of sex, the ecstasy on their faces, the sizes and shapes of the penises and breasts. She had returned them to the haphazard pile under Darrell's bed and fantasized in the dark.

That had been enough. M.J. had stayed in her fantasies, in the dark, a little shy and a little scared as the boys around her became men as their voices deepened and their shoulders broadened, but also curious, and although her fantasies were sexual, they were also loving and soft. She imagined her first time, as all girl-women do, as something beautiful.

A vein in her neck throbs. She imagines the sound of blood rushing through her body *powish powish* and then it surrounds her, and she knows the thumping and scratching didn't start in the kitchen. It started under her bed, inside her body. It had started with Jim. . . and the day he had stood up in church, a newcomer, and spewed his love of God over them with his straight white teeth. M.J. had slid further down into the pew, listless in her love of church or God, petulant and bored. Her mother and the Sisters in Christ ministry group had twittered like starlings in the treetops, scheming about which poor sister of God to pair him with.

A few Sundays later, M.J. had rolled over and fallen back asleep, chasing the edge of a dream. Rose had knocked and opened the door, huffing when she saw M.J. curled on her side. Her strident voice urged M.J. awake again.

"You're going to make us late. Ashley is ready to go."

"I don't wanna go."

"Well, you are. Get up!"

85

M.J. flung the bedsheets aside as she sat up.

"Darrell doesn't have to go, and Daddy doesn't go."

Pursing her lips, Rose put her hands on her hips.

"Do as I say, M.J. Get up and get dressed!"

Pouting, her arms crossed, M.J. felt her mother's anger pulsing over her throughout the sermon. Afterward, in the vestibule, Rose had spoken to Deacon Jim and his Christian white teeth, and he had graciously agreed to counsel M.J.

"Counsel her for what?" She'd heard her father ask that evening.

"She's becoming unmanageable, Hershel. This morning she was questioning why she had to go to church. That's the first step in falling away from the flock." Her mother was probably knitting and tapping her foot to some ethereal hymn. With her chin down, her eyes would have lifted to husband sitting in the faded, stained recliner, one arm worn threadbare where he picked at it as he watched football or baseball. M.J. could see her accusing gaze in her mind's eye, and although their voices dropped and she couldn't make out their words, their conversation was always the same.

"Don't look at me like that, Rose. I'm a good man, and I don't need God to tell me that."

"I know, Hershel, but good deeds won't get a man into heaven. Don't you want an eternal life at God's side?"

The first counseling sessions had been the same for M.J. Blah, blah, blah, rewind and repeat of every sermon she'd ever heard about the grace of God and the redemption of God. More than once her mind questioned whether God was a man, and why should God be a man instead of a woman when it was the woman who brought forth life onto the Earth? She thought of how magic was a sin, yet she can remember her wizened Uncle Delmer running his fingers over her hands, rubbing her warts, telling her about meeting a bear near his moonshine still until she forgot the sandpapery sensation of his wrinkled, cracked skin. A week later the warts had fallen off and never came back.

Her grandmother Muriel, her dad's mother for whom

86

she is named, heard an ethereal hymn as well, her foot tapping to its rhythm as she peeled apples for apple butter, her lips moving in silent prayer, praying without ceasing. Who could she be praying for so much? Yet, when M.J. saw her in the casket, her foot still, her lips pasted together, she felt a heaviness in her shoulders, and she knew then that it had been Grandma's prayers that had kept the weight away.

One afternoon, after her counseling, right before she had opened the door, Deacon Jim had run his hand down her hair and rubbed the small of her back. She skittered to the side, and when she looked at him, he had a funny smile on his face. At first his hand didn't move, just his fingers, then his hand brushed along the curve of her butt, and he kept talking as though it were nothing.

A confusing weight settled in M.J.'s mind, the right and the wrong of it, but something had jumped, jumped inside of her like a fish wrestling with a hook breaks the surface of a lake, then submerges itself again trying to run away from that hook, but only imbeds it deeper, and this fight is within the belly of the lake, the darkness, and leaves only ripples on the surface.

She had been ashamed for that involuntary jump, that misplaced desire, the traitorous flesh warring with an unwilling mind. She didn't even *like* Deacon Jim. His lips were full and rubbery looking, a little paunch around his middle, balding, and those teeth and his voice, that fucking preacher voice, televangelist preacher voice, revival preacher voice. He is the next best thing – youth minister, no certificate required, just the preacher voice.

The weight sat on M.J., sloping her shoulders as he sat ministering to her, his hand on her knee, then around her shoulders, brotherly, fatherly, friendly. Then his fingertips would brush the side of her breast and he would apologize, laugh it off, then stare at her as her nipples grew erect and sensitive, even as she crossed her arms over her chest. He would back off and sit across from her as she stared at the ground. Once she had seen him give his crotch a quick swipe, the bulge in it before he pulled his jacket closed. It all made her more curious, curious about the jumping fish and the tingle in her nipples, but she also felt disgusted and guilty for her reaction to him.

A month later the green curtains in his living room were drawn, the hot sun illuminating the edges. It made it darker than normal, and it was then he pulled her onto his lap and petted her hair, telling her how beautiful she was, his hand moving between her thighs, rubbing her through her shorts, his other hand sliding under her shirt, unclasping her bra while she sat confused, her chest tight, dizzy from shallow breaths.

"See what you do to me, M.J." The timber of his voice was not soothing, but accusatory. He shoved her down on the little couch and pushed her shirt up. His lips on her nipple made her gasp – shock, fear and. . . arousal. The fish plummeted into her core with paralyzing seduction and terror. She had lain suspended, uncomprehending, and in her confusion he devoured her, his hands sure as he slipped her shorts down.

"You're such a beautiful girl, M.J.," he panted, his chest hair gray and wiry. He unbuckled his belt. An electric pulse of adrenaline screamed through her veins, and said, "No." She struggled to sit up.

"No, Mr. Jim, no!"

He pushed her back down and held onto her shoulder, his finger digging into the little nerve under her collarbone, causing her to cry out. He panted harder, his pants down, his penis erect. He stroked it.

"See what you do to me? I can't help myself. All this time, M.J., you've been doing this to me." He tried to take her hand and force it onto him, but she pulled away and then he was on top of her, his hand between their bodies, between her legs, forcing them apart, his fingers pushing into her, his lips on her nipples. She pushed against his chest. She forgot how to breathe. She struggled. He was heavy. She felt something, his hand and something else. She braced against his chest and squirmed.

"No, no, I can't, I can't, stop."

"Yes, M.J., you have to. Feel what you do to me?" He rubbed against her, her vagina slick and ready, traitorous traitor. He had locked her against him, only her eyelashes and heart fluttering, her chest unable to rise.

"A man needs relief, M.J.," he said, pushing his penis into her. She stiffened and gasped, punching him, trying to squeeze her feet between them, to push him off, but he caught her wrists in one hand and smacked her with the other, the blow disorienting. Her head lolled back on the arm of the couch, and she detached.

She heard him talking, grunting, far away, "I can't help it." He moaned and collapsed, his prick jerking inside of her. She felt it as she stared at the chevron pattern in the ceiling, wondering if he were dead and wishing she was. She wanted to fall into the sky and drown in thin air, but he pulled out of her, and she lived.

He grasped her along the jawbone, his fingers tight, pain exploding through her temples.

"You wanted this, M.J. You've been seducing me every day, you and your little touches and your smile, making your nipples stand up through your shirt. I've seen it, I know you wanted me."

He forced her to her knees, her hair cloaking her shamed nakedness.

"You're a Jezebel. You have soiled us both, now pray."

She tried to pray, but her words were not what he wanted to hear. He jerked her up by her arm and hit her, his belt whisking with a practiced air across the back of her thighs, just once, just hard enough for more fear and more tears to cloud her vision, but not enough to hide the malice in his eyes as he stared down at her (dark demon rising), looming over her, and she shrunk back, shrunk down, confused, shamed, and terrified.

At home she sat in the shower, the scalding water raining like pellets of fire, gathering under her, rinsing away the rosy mist, soothing the soreness. She buried her stained panties in the garbage, wadding and knotting them to hide the brilliant red blood and his invisible smell.

Later, she sneaked onto the porch and sat in the rocking chair, its old wooden arms soft and smooth, marked alternately with impetigo and age spots. The darkness was moist and busy – bullfrogs lowed, their throats pregnant, crickets chirped and somewhere an errant blind cicada sang *zreeeuh zreeeuh zreeeuh* to its sleeping companions. She drew her knees under her chin, her nightgown sticking to her skin, and in that busy, moist night the Peeling Paint House shuddered, as though uprooting itself, and swayed, and rocked the chair which rocked her until she slept.

Now, she runs her splayed hands down her taut stomach, tests the weight of her breasts, and knows her dear house is infected, as surely as boll weevils infest cotton and smut mars the corn, they are infected.

The haint floats between the walls, light as tendrils of smoke, feeding on anxiety and guilt, morphing and writhing, wicked in its power. It can see in all directions without eyes, hear feelings without heart or soul or ears. Nothing is sacred or hidden from its thirst, its unquenchable hunger for the pain and confusion of the malcontent. Tiny claws expand and contract from its mist, and it clings between the mirrors of the girl-woman and her mother. Neither realizing that as they stare at their own reflections, they also stare at one another. But the haint knows and watches and feeds.

Rose combs her hair, her eyes dissecting each gray strand, the sag at the underside of her breasts, even erect her nipples not as pert. After three children, the skin over her stomach is no longer taut and silver lines of stretch marks shine in the light.

She notices with satisfaction that the gray is not as noticeable since she clipped her pubic hair, like he likes it. Feeling a familiar twinge she rubs lower, eyelids shuttering over dark eyes as she manipulates her clitoris, legs apart, a feral grunt in her throat, remembering the last time she had seen him.

Jim's door had opened before she could knock, and M.J. pushed passed her, books tight against her chest, as sullen as before.

"You should wait in the car while I talk to your mother," he said, and M.J.'s head had snapped around.

As Rose's voice echoed his, Jim closed the door and waited a moment before bending and kissing her. M.J.'s counseling was just another reason to see him. The Wednesday prayer meetings were growing longer and longer, at least for her. The first time he touched her, he apologized, then stared at her with a longing like Hershel no longer did.

"I can't help myself," he said.

Back and forth she went in ecstasy and guilt. She found herself living in fantasies of a life without Hershel, without Darrell and M.J. and their teenage petulance. She would take Ashley with her. The child deserved an opportunity, opportunities that had already passed for her. You have to catch them young. That's what Jim said as he stroked her hair, her neck, her breasts, down her belly, blinding her to her daughter's red face, her stunned silence, her pain, her shame.

She hears water running in the bathroom, the uneven splashes as coal dust and earth run from her husband's body, dirty water swirling in a single eddy, pulling the waste away. Rose shudders as the shower stops, her senses heightened, gathering together like the water drops, dripping and pattering like tiny footsteps. She wonders what her husband would think if she were to continue standing before the mirror, naked, her hand between her legs, pleasuring herself. They have sex every Saturday night, and that was enough for him, but for her, she wants more. Rose needs him to touch her. Now she has someone to touch her, and she doesn't care what anyone says, not even God.

The thump comes between the two, the girl-woman and her mother, both jerking their hands away from their bodies. The scratching starts again. *Sccccccrreak sccccccrrreak sccccccrrreak* M.J. bends and presses her ear against the wall. It thumps, and she stifles a scream and fights her way into her nightclothes, then whirls, pulls the door open, and steps out, meeting Rose in the hallway. A heartbeat follows *thump-thump, thump-thump* as they glower at one another. The heartbeat fades, meanders down the hallway and dissipates.

"Go to bed," Rose says.

M.J. feels she is caught in an inescapable snare. She plods through the remainder of summer, punctuated by counseling sessions, and sometimes she sits in her mother's rattling Buick and looks at her in silent angst at what awaits her within Jim's house, but her mother cannot hear her silent thoughts, M.J. cannot open her silent mouth, and it seems as though her mother is lost in her own silence, but is happy in it.

When M.J. locks herself in the bathroom of Werner High School, its stalls scrawled with teenage love and hate, it is alone. She has not even told her best friend, Katie, a willowy blond with short curly hair and the funniest laugh M.J.'s ever heard. She has wanted to tell Katie. She has wanted to answer when Katie asks what is wrong with her. She shuffles to and from classes, her head in her books, and sometimes the teachers catch her daydreaming and shake their heads. She used to be such a good student.

When she pees on the stick, there is nowhere to lay it flat like the directions say, so with her panties around her ankles, M.J. stays seated on the toilet, the test flat across her hands, and watches the urine climb up the absorbent tip and disappear into the plastic before reappearing in the results window. She stays there for a long time, until her hips ache. Finally, she stands, wraps the test and the little plus sign in toilet paper, and throws it in the garbage.

When M.J. tells Jim, he beats her, his fists, his belt, leaving welts and bruises, her scalp burning as he pulls her hair.

"You're a whore," he says, "Muriel Jezebel. Who's responsible for this?"

Her lips tremble around her gaping mouth, tears dripping and spreading along her gums.

"You are," she whispers.

Leaning in close, their noses almost touching, his eyes hard in his piggish face, he snarls,

"How dare you accuse me of such a thing when it was you who came in here and slutted yourself before me, tempting me until I couldn't control myself, and then expect me to believe that I'm the only one that you've tempted, that you've spread your legs for!"

M.J. stands away from herself, frozen, her voice pleading and begging, the slaps and pinches, they must have hurt, but his curled lip, the hate spewing from his mouth creating a dark dust in the room, an ebony aura pulsing with a heartbeat, red and orange, and she sees the demon within him, rising. He shakes her by the neck (dark demon rising), and she hears a comforting *shush shush shush* like a rocking chair on carpet (pray without ceasing) that drowns his words (red demon rising) *shush shush shush* (pray without ceasing) the crying child, the drowning girl-woman. Oh, I must be dying. The crying child hitches, her soul returns to dark spots swimming and pain explodes, and she explodes with pain.

She kicks him in the groin and the *shush* subsides. She runs. Her hand fumbles on the doorknob, and she hears him behind her. She runs into the woods, away, where he cannot, will not, follow. Her flushed boiling skin chills in the late autumn air, water leaks into her shoes from stagnate soggy backwaters, tree skeletons piercing the waxy (half moon rising), and she slips on the steep bank before climbing onto the gravel edge of the road. A loud muffler and a pair of headlights wind their way to her. She rubs her arms as the car stops. The window lowers with a creak and her brother's friend Jake looks out at her. Darrell leans over the steering wheel.

"What are you doing?"

"Goin' home."

"Get in the car. Where's your jacket and shit?"

"I forgot it, tried to take a shortcut."

Looking in the rearview mirror as the dome light fades, Darrell sees a wildness, a fear, a trapped fear that animals get. Her nose is red, and he does not know if it is from crying or from the cold.

"What the fuck happened? You been at the preacher guy's?"

"He's not a preacher."

"Who?" Jake asks.

"Deacon Jim," she answers.

Darrell doesn't say anything more, but he keeps looking in the rear view mirror at her. M.J. looks out the window, remembering now what he'd said.

"No one will believe you. They all know you're a whore! You're trouble and a liar! A liar! You find someone, Muriel Jane, you find that someone responsible, because it isn't me! It isn't me!"

M.J. sidles around the corner of the lockers, her books tight against her chest. Jake notices her and lifts his chin. He has bad acne along his jaw and there's a tiny piece missing from his left front tooth where it was clipped clean by a knuckle in a fist fight. She knows, and has known, he likes her. He always smiles at her, opens doors with a grand flourish, and asks her to all of the dances. Until now, she had been afraid, too shy, and now she is too afraid not to approach him. Maybe she has always wanted to, but she should not. He is too good, too sweet, and she backs around the corner, desperate to disappear. She is trying. Her hipbones rub against her jeans, her cheekbones protrude, deepening the sockets of her eyes. She does not realize this, she only knows she wishes she could blow away in the wind like a wisp of smoke. Yet, he finds her.

"Hey, M.J."

"Hey."

He leans against the locker, one finger hooked in his jeans' pocket, and scrapes his straight brown bangs out of his eyes.

"You going to the dance Friday?"

"Maybe."

"You wanna go with me?"

She hears herself say yes, and watches the fish jump in his eyes, hears the excitement in his voice before he leans against the locker again, cool and contained. But she knows that fish, and she knows it is swimming around and around inside of him.

Two weeks later the suspension squeaks as Jake's old car, one of many his dad, Jake Sr., keeps around the gas station, bumps along the rutted road, skirting giant mud holes worn deep and dangerous by vintage trucks with lift kits and bad transmissions.

"Don't worry, M.J., she'll hold together."

M.J. is not worried about being swallowed into one of the muddy lakes. She has already been swallowed by the whale, and inside it is dark and moist, and she is the fetus floating in the womb, though she is without a comforting hand, the invisible love from without.

"You okay?"

"I'm fine."

"I mean, you haven't said much."

She feels sorry for him. She thought this would be hard, being with him, wanting him, but he looks at her with softness, like she is something special.

And I am nothing but a Jezebel.

Their pupils are wide, drinking in the light of the dashboard. He smooths out her hair, touching her face, her lips, but he does not push her, he rests, slumping a little lower in the seat, like he is deciding something.

"I know a place, you know, like a little hunting cabin up on the ridge. Won't be hard to get to, has heat," he shrugs, "If you want to."

"I do," she says, and he grins.

"Yeah?"

"Yeah."

The cabin is a tangle of clapboard, plywood and particle board, the steps squeaking as he leads her up them and inside. A chain jangles and creates a swinging shadow on the wall as the bare bulb illuminates the room. An old stove sits in the middle, coal fed at one time, now Jake rummages with plywood cast offs and yellowed newspapers. There is a cot covered with a bright quilt against one wall, and a small table with three mismatched chairs sits close to the stove. It only has one window, and there are still triangles of wood wedged into the frame for stability.

Leaving the door to the stove open, he reaches up and pulls the chain. M.J. closes her eyes and opens them again, still just seeing his shadow against the flickering flames. She steps closer to him, closer to the flames. His chest hair sprouts from the V in his shirt, dark and curly. M.J. touches it, fascinated by its softness and the way it curves in the hollow of his throat. She feels the thud-skip of his heart when she lays her hand on his chest, hears the shallow quick breaths as she unbuttons his shirt, but his hands move slow and soft along her arms, then her breasts, the curve of her hip, his tongue sliding into her mouth. The first tremor of real desire, desire without revulsion, desire without shame, moves her to stand closer and throw her arms around him.

"We don't have to, M.J.," he says. She does not know why he said it until she feels wetness on her cheeks.

"I want to." (I have to find someone responsible)

He frowns and catches her hand as she traces the swell and recess of his stomach. His hand is large with long tapered fingers, calloused, nails bitten to the quick. Hers is soft and small, nails bitten to the quick.

"Then why are you crying?"

"Because, you're beautiful."

And I'm a traitorous traitor, a lying Jezebel.

Darrell slows and parks the car in a wide spot beside the road. The muffler has a hole and sounds like a pack of Harleys. He has already cruised past that damn preacher man's house four times, and each time his mother's Buick is still parked there. His dad is on the hoot owl shift and the Wednesday prayer meeting is going long, if they are even praying. He never liked the looks of that man, and after seeing his sister's face two weeks ago, he likes him even less, and his mother, goddamn her, she beat M.J. with a belt after M.J. ran out on her "counseling."

He could not hear everything, just snatches, but enough to know M.J. stood firm despite the beating, and she had not gone back to the not-preacher. Now that she is seeing Jake, she seems happier, nicer, not tied up in knots, even with that fucking haint crashing and banging all the damn time. He wishes she would gain some weight. It is painful to look across the dinner table at her gaunt face. Something is off, different, just wrong, just fucking wrong. He leans against a towering sycamore, its skin cool and white. His shoulders hunch against the fall breeze, which is different than any other breeze because it brings a hint of sun, leaf mold, and old rain in its bouquet, and he breathes it deep, savoring it. It is more than an hour before the door opens. They look around, using only their eyes to see, before a final kiss, and that is all he needs. As he watches her car drive away, the wind shifts, and its stench is now just the bitterness of winter.

"What happened to you?"

Jake traces a welt on her back. M.J. flinches and pulls her shirt over her head, yanking it down over her torso, then crosses her arms.

"I thought they were all gone."

97

Jake squats in front of her, his hands on her knees.

"Was it your mom? Darrell said she's hard on you."

M.J. shrugs, "It's okay."

Jake looks down at the floor between her legs noticing how she puts one foot on top of the other.

"M.J., if somebody's hurting you. . ."

"Nobody's hurting me! Just leave it alone, Jake."

He looks at her down-turned face, her eyes on her clasped hands and knows she is lying. He rubs her knees and stands up.

"Okay."

Time ticks. M.J. hears it in the walls and under the floorboards, sometimes even when the haint is quiet, when it hides, she hears the ticking. At night, the haint wails under the front porch, thumps, growls, and paces just out of sight, and no one sleeps.

Ashley is scared. She putters with Darrell in the garage, handing him the wrong tools until she exhausts his patience and he sends her away. She is afraid to sleep at night, afraid the haint is under her bed. Although it seems to like her the least, she is not immune from the crashings and smashings in the middle of the night. It sounds like it will tear right through the wall. Sometimes she switches on the light and watches until the floorboards begin to swim before her eyes, and it is just the illusion they are moving and rising.

The first time she had screamed, and her mother had come running into the room, then Rose had whipped her for waking the house for nothing. Ashley waits, staring at the ceiling, afraid to look around, startling at every sound, terrified. It laughs, a soft evil chortle right behind her head, and she cries silent tears that drip down the sides of her face into her ears. Then she hears footsteps, human, and trying very hard to be quiet. The bolt slips with a click, and Ashley blinks away tears, a darker gray of shadow in her doorway.

"Ashley?" It is the lightest whisper, like a breeze

rustling a flower petal.

"Yeah?" Ashley is not as gentle, as quiet, as soft, and the figure comes into the room.

"It's okay," M.J. whispers, "I'm here."

Ashley clings to her, "It laughed at me. It laughed, I think, because I'm scared."

"I believe you," M.J. says, rocking her, "I believe you."

M.J. hears a different sound now, and her eyes, even in darkness, seek the movement, seek to compartmentalize, to categorize that *sound*. She recognizes it and hugs Ashley tighter. It frightens her more than any other sound it has ever made. It is skipping.

Ashley stands in the doorway of M.J.'s room.

"Mom wanted me to look through your old stuff in the closet."

"What do you want? T-shirt? Shorts?"

"No, Mom said I need a bra," Ashley whispers the last word, her arms cross over her chest, embarrassed and possibly bewildered.

"Did you get your period yet?"

Ashley shakes her head.

"My friend Niki got hers though. Is it really bad?"

M.J. almost says, only if you don't get it, but instead she says, "It's okay. Sometimes the cramps are a bitch."

M.J. opens the door to the closet and pulls a garbage bag out. She digs through it until she finds an older, smaller bra which she breezed through in a few months. The elastic is still good.

"Try it on."

Ashley's eyes widen.

"I'll turn my back," M.J. says.

After a moment, Ashley says, "I hate it."

M.J. adjusts the straps.

"Is that better?"

"Yeah, thanks."

Ashley puts her shirt on and crosses her arms again. M.J. hugs her.

M.J. catches up to her father as he clears his things from the front seat of his truck. She takes his lunch pail and waits for him to shut the door. It creaks and scrapes with rust, making her fingernails curl. They walk up the driveway.

"You doing all right, Muriel?"

M.J. glances at him and sees coal dust caught in the creases of his eyes, the fine straight nose and blue eyes that she inherited, the slight limp from an old injury.

"I'm okay, Dad."

She walks several more steps before realizing he has stopped.

"You look just like your grandma."

He says it so often she wonders how bad he must miss her. (Pray without ceasing)

Something is wrong with his girl. Something is different. Hell, something is different with all of them, and every night that damn haint starts its racket. No, not just at night anymore, it's a brazen little fucker.

It's just an old saying, meant to scare kids into minding their parents. It's an animal caught under the house, mice between the walls. He found some arrowheads when they cleared the area around the old barn. Maybe it was Indian spirits. Once, he looked over, across the creek, and saw a line of them coming down the mountainside, the road gone, the creek running in a different place. He stared and stared until his eyes watered, and when he blinked and looked again, they were gone.

The mountains are full of mystery. A man can search a lifetime and never understand the turn of the poplar leaf when it's ready to rain. It was something you were born into, the old ways, the superstitions, the magic of removing warts and curing thrush, of sitting up with the dead and knowing by smelling the wind that it has frosted for the last time. Yes, it is a way of knowing, like a seed planted that continues to grow, its roots snaking deeper and deeper into the hollows, the creek, and the sky like a blue river between the peaks of the hills, reflecting back into the creek until all that is or was, is water and sky and earth, and if it could tilt and turn you would never know which way was up.

"Daddy?"

Hershel shakes his head and blinks. M.J. stares at him as he realizes he has been staring at her without seeing. The wind gusts and leaves fall like snow. Whatever is happening, they are losing.

The Peeling Paint House awakens, but is slow coming to consciousness. She is old and fatigued, her bones are a little more brittle and arthritic, she creaks in places she didn't before. Her foundation has developed deep wrinkles from the blasting at a nearby surface mine, but within, the Peeling Paint House is resolute with purpose, the purpose she had been built with - to protect the family within. She had known other haints before, but none so strong and draining as this one. It is becoming easier to drift into slumber in the mid-afternoon sun, to doze before the chilling winds of winter sweep through the hollow, before the frost breathes on the windows, before the snow clings to the roof and the eaves and melts and drips into jagged icicles.

She senses the presence of the woman, the mother, the grandmother, who takes her place in the rocking chair and taps her foot, her lips still moving in silent prayer (pray without ceasing). If one were to see the rocking chair rocking, they would think of wind, not spirit. The Peeling Paint House and the rocking chair are old friends, the silent protectors and comforters of this family, and this is why the old woman returns, to watch, to protect, to comfort, but all of them are old, weary, and useless.

Jake hooks M.J.'s bangs behind her ear.

"You look tired."

Slamming her locker door, M.J. turns to him.

"It's the haint. It won't leave us alone."

Jake laughs.

"You don't really believe that shit, do you? It's an old wives tale, just mountain folk talking," his smile fades at the look on her face. Her eyes are hard, her mouth set and obstinate.

"It's real, Jake, and it's evil," she whispers. Jake stuffs his hands in the pockets of his jeans.

"What are you gonna do?"

M.J. looks away, over his shoulder, between their feet, but not at him.

"I don't know yet."

He trundles her books under his arm and takes her hand. They walk down the hall, and only one of them knows the haint isn't the only thing she doesn't know about.

The bed trembles. M.J. flops to her side, pulling the pillow over her head. The haint wails and screeches like an owl, only angry, angry and restless and hateful. The scratching intensifies into a thousand tiny claws and a thousand tiny sharp teeth, clawing and gnawing their way through the walls to devour her. The ticking never stops.

M.J. comes into the kitchen, the smell of food turns her stomach but she spoons some onto her plate and sits down. Darrell is already there.

"Where's Ashley?"

"She's helping Deacon Jim with the new youth group," Rose says.

M.J. jumps to her feet, "You have to go get her."

"What's wrong with you?" Rose asks. M.J. doesn't answer, instead she turns to Darrell.

"Will you take me to get her?"

There it is again, that trapped feral look she had the night he found her beside the road. He lays his fork down.

"I'll take you."

"No, you're not. Sit down, M.J. I'll pick up Ashley after while," Rose says.

"It'll be too late after while!" M.J. runs her hands through her hair, "We have to go now! We have to, right now, right now, Mom."

"You're just not making any sense!" Rose grabs M.J.'s hands and M.J. pulls away, flicking her fingers and shaking her head.

"Is one of us not enough? You have to send both of us to him? She's just a baby!"

"What are you talking about? He wants her to help with the youth group."

M.J. shakes her head again, imagining him seducing Ashley with lies, his hands, his lips, his cock. God! Where are you? (dark demon rising)

"That's not what he wants," M.J. advances on her, fists clenched at her sides, "He wants to fuck her, just like he fucked me!"

Rose blanches and smacks M.J.'s face. Darrell jumps up, his fists clenched, but speechless. What did she say? No. No. NO.

"You," Rose points, "Are a liar! He warned me about how manipulative you are."

M.J. burst into tears, "I'm not lying!"

The haint attacks the floor, the table legs thumping, a violent feral scream rends the air, and the scratching crawls over them like lice.

"It knows I'm not lying! It knows!" M.J. sobs. Rose grabs the edge of the table which has begun to march across the floor.

"Shut up! Shut up!" Rose screams.

Darrell points at his mother.

"No! Don't take up for him! I know what you've done!"

M.J. looks from one to the other, tremulous and sick.

"What? What did she do?"

There is a sudden silence as even the haint stops to

listen. A water droplet from the leaking faucet that no one cares to fix, gathers, pulling its energy into a point that releases and drips into a discarded coffee cup, plopping with a low murmur that vibrates through all of them.

"He's just starting his own little harem, isn't he, Mom?" Darrell comes around the table, "M.J., you, and now Ashley! When's it going to stop?"

Rose gyrates her head back and forth, "No, no, no!"

"Yes!" Darrell slams his fist on the table, "That's what it is! I saw you kiss him!"

M.J.'s mouth drops open, and she rushes to cover it with her hands even as a piercing wail forces its way from deep inside of her, and then the haint begins bouncing, merry and joyful beneath their feet.

M.J.'s hands separate like claws, "Did you know? Did you know what he was doing to me!"

Hershel opens the door to a cacophony of screeching, banging, and crying. He slams the moving table to the floor.

"What the hell!"

M.J. looks at her mother, but Rose looks at the floor, and it is Darrell who turns and says, "We need to go get Ashley."

"That don't tell me nothing. Where is she?"

"She's with Deacon Jim," M.J. says, "He'll hurt her, Daddy."

He waits for her to say it, to say, "like he hurt me," because he can see it, he can feel it (dark demon rising). That's it, right in front of him, this truth he can barely stand. There are only so many ways a man can hurt a woman, and his little girl stands in front of him crying, trembling, her head bowed, shame in the slump of her shoulders, and his wife won't look at him. He curls his lip at her.

"Rose?" She jerks her head and looks at him.

There are things a man knows that can't be taught – how the wind smells after the last frost, how the poplar leaf turns before it rains, the magic of removing warts and curing thrush, and the look in a woman's eyes when she has stepped out on her man, when she has failed to protect his heart, his home, and his children.

The haint follows him to the bedroom, its evil skittering claws scratching the walls from within, and as Hershel picks up the baseball bat from the corner behind the door, he slams into the wall.

"Shut up!"

When he returns to the kitchen, Darrell says, "I'll go with you." No one has moved, but now Rose shakes her head.

"What are you going to do?"

Hershel chokes up on the bat and slaps it into the palm of his hand, like the haint slaps against the floor, against the walls, books falling from shelves, a screen door slamming.

"I'm going to make this right."

The truck engine ticks in the cold and Darrell gets out first, fumbling in the bed for the rusted tire iron his dad refuses to replace.

"You're not going," Hershel says. Darrell rests his forearms on the edge of the truck.

"I am, Dad. I'm going with you."

Hershel shakes his head, realizing he isn't a boy anymore. It hurts, but he's still his boy.

"You get Ashley, and you take her home, then you come back for me."

Rose and M.J. circle each other, wary, stunned, and angry.

"I want that tea you made for Aunt Mary."

Shaking her head, Rose asks, "What tea?"

"Don't pretend like you don't know," M.J. sneers at her, "I know what you did."

Rose raises her chin, "Why? That tea is dangerous. There are things you don't know."

"It's only dangerous for women who are preg-nant, moth-er," M.J.'s eyes flash, "I know more than you think I do."

Lowering her face into her hands, Rose shakes her head, "No, no, you're not!"

"I am," M.J. says, "And you're going to help me get rid of it."

Rose cries, "It's that boy's baby!"

"It's not! And if I wait any longer it won't work," M.J. advances on her, "You owe me," she says. A giggle ripples along the frame of the house, and M.J. slaps the wall with her open palm.

"Shut up!"

Rose wipes her hands on her skirt, then turns and opens the cabinet.

"Hi, Darrell," Ashley says, looking up from her seat at Jim's kitchen table. The deacon stands to the side of the open door.

"Evening, Darrell. I wasn't expecting you."

"I guess not, Deacon. Ashley, get your stuff, we gotta go."

Ashley gathers her books and the lamb the deacon had given her and goes into the dark, pausing at the threshold until Darrell takes her hand.

Jim watches Darrell and Ashley drive away. He sees a dark shadow approaching in his peripheral vision and he is not surprised when Hershel steps onto the porch.

"We need to talk, Deacon."

Jim doesn't ask why he's there or what he may have to talk to him about. There are things a man knows, and what Jim knows is that he never should have come here, should have never brought his sickness, but this man, this man doesn't know that. I am a man of God, Jim convinces himself. Hershel is here for redemption, and so Jim walks into the house, ready to give it. That's what this is about. Hershel is an ignorant sinner. Rose has told Jim everything. What he has done, he has done for the good.

Jim turns as the door closes, and when he sees the

baseball bat, the smile around his straight white teeth fades. There are things a man knows. This is not about redemption. It's about justice. Dropping to his knees, Jim begins to pray.

"Oh, Lord, I have sinned. . .," and Hershel swings the bat.

M.J. sits on her bed, sipping from a mug. The pungent odor of the tea assails her nose, settles into her pores, and she feels no fear or remorse.

Deep in the forest, off the bumpy dirt road, close to the disjointed hunting cabin, but not within a stone's throw, is an old ventilation shaft, a discard of a mine that breached a spring, and under its rusty forgotten lid lays Deacon Jim (dark demon dead) in the still, frigid damp of the underground. The sound of the hacksaw's *shush shush shush* is comforting to Darrell as his dad cuts up the bat and throws the pieces onto the fire, their shadows leaking into the trees and dissipating at the end of the reach of the flames.

Hershel washes his hands, looks in the mirror, and sees his wife behind him.

"What have you done?"

"What a man should do, Rose. My conscience is clear. Maybe you should go pray and clear yours."

Rose starts crying and whispers, "I'm sorry."

Rose stares at the coffee grounds in the bottom of her empty mug as though looking for an answer in their muddy scrawls until her sister Mary disturbs them with a fresh pour.

"You're not the only one, ya know?" Mary says as she sits down, "I heard that man has been. . . "

"I know," Rose says, cutting her off, "But what about M.J.?"

"M.J. will be fine."

"What if the tea doesn't work?"

"It worked for me, for you, God knows for how many

other women since Grandma Combs first did it, even if she was the first."

"But Hershel. . . "

"Hershel did what was right, just like we did with the snakes."

Rose leans back in the chair, closes her eyes, and exhales. Their daddy had been a Pentacostal, a snake handler. One Sunday their mother had stayed home with their younger brother, and Mary and Rose had been in the basement of the church, the raucous foot stomping, preaching, and praying seeping down via the open stairs, until a sudden silence made them look up. There was a faulty long note on a guitar, then murmurs, and hurried footsteps on the stairs. Darnell Hager slid into the doorway.

"Where's Rose?" And nine year old Rose had raised her hand.

"Your daddy's been bit. Where's your mom?"

When Rose said she was at home with Ricky, Darnell had bustled her into the car and driven her there, telling her he would wait until they came out. Rose had run into the house, letting the screen door slam, which normally she would be whipped for, and yelled for her mom. Thinking her mom and Ricky might be napping, she went to her parents' room and opened the door without knocking. Her mother was buttoning her house dress and there was a strange man in the bed. He was propped up against the headboard, hands laced behind his head, and in his curly black hair, black eyes, and pug nose, Rose saw herself.

"What is it?" Her mother snapped.

"Daddy's been bit," Rose said. She couldn't take her eyes from the man in the bed, even when he reared his head back and laughed.

"Your preacher man got bit, Wanda. The serpent got Moses today!"

Rose didn't know what he meant. Her daddy's name wasn't Moses, it was Floyd.

"Goddamnit, shut up, William Lee!"

Having never heard her mother cuss before, Rose's mouth dropped open.

"You done scared the hell outta my baby girl," he said.

"I said shut up!" Wanda grabbed Rose's arm and drug her out of the room, her fingers tight around Rose's wrist. Before they got to the front door, Wanda jerked Rose to a stop and tugged at the tiny hairs at the base of her skull, enough to bring tears to Rose's eyes.

"Don't say nothin' about what you saw or heard. You understand me, girl?"

Rose had stared, and her mother had slapped her, then shook her by the shoulders.

"I asked you if you understood me?"

"Yes, Ma'am!"

As they were going outside, Rose looked back and saw the man standing in the doorway of the bedroom, his arms crossed over his naked chest, and her mother closed the door on William "Moonshine Bill" Mullins. Rose was sure her mother had been sleeping with the devil. The snake that bit her daddy wasn't just a snake, but *the* serpent, the same serpent that had tempted Eve, the same serpent this man had sent, and even as they arrived at the church and joined the other congregants in a laying on of hands, anointment and prayer, even as her father breathed his last, Rose knew what she had to do.

As the undertaker's arrival took everyone's attention, Rose grabbed Mary and told her that one of the snakes wasn't really a snake, but *the* serpent, and seven year old Mary had blinked through her tears, so stunned she didn't hesitate to follow Rose to the pulpit and carry one of the snake boxes outside, anxious rattling erupting from within.

"No, turn it over," Rose had said when Mary started to set the box on the ground, "Turn it over onto the air holes."

And that was how they killed the snakes that killed their daddy, but that wasn't the last time Rose would see Moonshine Bill, nor the last time he would claim she was his baby girl. There really was no denying it, after all, she looked just like most of Bill's other children, including Ricky, but not Mary. Through the years, she and Mary had come to accept this, but it didn't mean that Rose didn't mourn and miss the man she had called "Daddy." Lord knows Moonshine Bill didn't know a thing about being a father, and Wanda didn't know a thing about keeping her legs shut, which is how Rose and Mary learned about the tea. Each had had their taste of the tea, Rose at fifteen for her own indiscretions, and Mary just the year before, both more like their mother than they cared to admit.

Rose exhales again and opens her eyes. Mary stirs another teaspoon of sugar into her coffee and says,

"Let it go, Rosa Lee, let it go."

"Darrell came to pick me up, and then we came home," Ashley says and shrugs. Her dark eyes are clear and bright, honest. Deputy Joe Thornhill slaps his knees and stands, setting his hat on his head.

"I appreciate you all talking to me."

"Sorry we couldn't help you more," Hershel says, shaking Joe's hand.

"Damnedest thing I've ever seen, Hershel. I'd love to know what happened to that man. Mrs. Willis was real shook up, finding his house like that. You know," Joe says, turning at the last moment, "I've heard rumors, rumors he wasn't that great of a guy."

Hershel sticks his hands in his pockets, "I don't go to church, Joe. I mind my own business."

Joe nods.

"Take care."

"Will do."

"Oh, Joe," Rose steps onto the porch, "How's Jessie Lee?"

"She's doing real good. I'm sure she'd like to hear from ya."

"I might do that."

Joe had heard that before, both from Rose and his

girlfriend, but neither could seem to bridge the gap Bill Mullins left in their lives, the known and the unknown.

After Hershel and Rose step back in and shut the door, Joe stops and looks back at the house. He had been there before. He had, for a brief time, dated Hershel's sister, Jacquetta, and that house gave him the creeps. It was like it was alive. After one evening, when he heard footsteps when nobody was there, he never went back. Even now it seems the house is watching him. He shakes his head, gets in the cruiser and pulls away, happy to be gone.

Ashley sits on her bed holding the lamb Deacon Jim gave her. She didn't tell Deputy Thornhill about the man she saw. She wasn't even sure it was a man she saw in the side mirror as Darrell drove them away. Now she believes she saw the devil with his pitchfork, or maybe just a moon shadow. Moon shadows always make things bigger. She also isn't sure how she feels about what happened to Deacon Jim. At first, she liked him, until that last day when he had given her the lamb. He put his arm around her, brotherly, fatherly, friendly. He squeezed her tighter and stroked her hair. It scared her.

She picks the lamb up, tosses it into the deep corner of her closet, and shuts the door. She doesn't feel bad about it. From behind her, she hears a faint, "Awww," as though someone, or something, is deeply disappointed.

M.J. lies on her side, her knees drawn to her chest. She had barely been able to hide her discomfort from Deputy Thornhill. It has been three days, and she suffers until the urge cannot be denied. She sits on the toilet, her face in her hands, trembling, and as the first scarlet drop of blood drips into the water, she thinks, my conscience is clear.

The haint grumbles and rumbles then evaporates. The Peeling Paint House shudders, like a dog shaking off fleas, and is whole again.

Pile Up

Look here y'all, last fall I was over at my great aunt Mamie's place. Like the rest of the Mullinses, Mamie has white hair, I mean white-white, but she don't want you to know that. She'd gotten the skunk stripe so I went over on my day off and dyed her hair. Then we sat down on her front porch to shell some beans she'd dried out over the winter. Mamie's house sits right in the middle of a straight stretch, and by straight stretch I mean a place where the road is straight and flat enough for one car to pass a coal truck going Mach two. That's a passing zone in these parts.

Me and Mamie are shooting the shit and gossiping when I hear a roaring sound. I look up and see headlights and flashers coming around the curve. Well, that time of day, about eleven, the only reason for headlights and flashers is a funeral procession. I was about to say something to Mamie when her old ears caught the roaring sound, and she looked over her shoulder. Good thing she did or she would have missed the whole thing because a yellow flash whips out of the funeral procession and guns the engine. Holy shit, now! I ain't never seen anybody with enough balls to pass a funeral procession, much less in *the short bus*. You heard me right! The goddamn short bus is passing a funeral procession! If that wasn't enough, well, one of those coal trucks going Mach two, yeah, it just came around the other curve – fully loaded – or in these parts – overloaded.

I can assure you there was a collective, Oh shit! Now, you're probably imagining this didn't turn out so good. Let's just say it turned out better than it could have. One good thing is that there's a ditch that runs along the edge of the road. That's where the coal truck went, into the ditch, and he was riding it like a three dollar whore. Problem is that ditch ends at Mamie's driveway, which is just a concrete slab over a drainage pipe. Boy, did he hit it! It sounded like a coal truck hitting a concrete bridge and dumping its load. Sure did. And that was just what was happening on our side of the road.

I got a good look as the bus rocketed by us. That would be Percy Nelson driving. He looked a little panicked. This, my friends, is what happens when the lunatics are in charge of the asylum. I went to school with Percy and one day he came to school with his right eye all taped over. Seems he'd had a fight with a toothbrush. It takes a special kind of stupid to almost put your own eye out while you're brushing your teeth. Plus, he almost choked to death in shop class when the strings from his hoodie got hung up in one of the machines. Instead of just wiggling out of the hoodie, he let it drag him all the way up the belt until his face turned purple. And who in their right mind continues to eat their own boogers after kindergarten? Percy. You'd be sitting in class and he'd be sunk up to his knuckle mining for gold. As you can imagine, this made him a hit with the ladies. Still turns my stomach.

Bet you're wondering how they could put someone without a lick of common sense in charge of the special kids. Well, it's because his family are big in politics, and if one of their own wants a job, then they get a job. It don't matter much to them that he's still eats his own boogers, and if the rumors are right, smears his tallywacker with peanut butter so his dog will give him a blow job. I tell ya, working at the bar has lowered my IQ since I'm forced to listen to this crazy shit.

Anywho, Percy tried to jet back into the right lane and clipped the hearse's front fender. The hearse hit the gravel on the side of the road and spun out, the car behind it almost hit it broadside, and that roaring sound, it was fifty bikers that started slipping and sliding all over the road and piling up on each other, and the other twenty or so cars in the procession and four empty coal trucks behind them with their air brakes squalling and their tires bouncing and stuttering. Now, as if all of this ain't bad enough, I looked over and saw something. . . different. No shit. That coal truck driver wasn't the only one who dumped his load. The fucking coffin was lying on the

113

side of the road, the lid had popped open, and from where I was standing, I could see the dearly departed all jumbled up in there. I guess they don't belt them in.

Here's another bit of bad news. The dearly departed was Ragin' Rod Asbury, Vice-President of the Brothers of the Wheel, hence the fifty motorcycles. I saw Rod's widow get out of the car behind the hearse. That would be Midge. Her real name is Martha, but everyone calls her Midge, short for midget. Midge is only about yay-tall, which is somewhere on the underside of five feet. There's only one thing God gave Midge and that was a bad attitude. I swear if the woman ever smiled her face would crack, plus, she puts Mamie to shame in the dyed hair department. I don't figure though that Midge knows what hair dye is because it looks like she uses shoe polish or shellac. It's slicked back and cut straight across the bottom like a helmet, but her hair bleeds onto her forehead where she keeps a wisp of bangs. I've always wanted to try and wipe it off with a gob of spit, just to see if I could. Midge would probably bite me, plus she's so ugly I keep expecting a house to fall on her.

Midge also has this way about her where she has to have constant reassurance that you understand what she wants. As in, she punctuates every sentence with "Are ya following me?" And she's real hateful about it, like you're the dumbest person she's ever seen. "I need a beer, are ya following me?" "I need another beer, are ya following me?" "Rod needs another shot, are ya following me?" And when she got really drunk, "I need to go to the bathroom, are ya following me?" No, I ain't following you to the bathroom, you drunk, ugly hussy, not unless it's with a roll of duct tape.

I saw the funeral director, you know, my Rastafarian undertaker brother-in-law, Max Anderson, the one married to my sister Sugar Ray, with a hand on his forehead. He was wearing a standard black suit with a yellow tie, a yellow handkerchief, and I bet there was even a yellow pinstripe in his pants. He's tall and thin with long arms, long legs, and yes, even long fingers that he was waving around towards the

114

funeral home flunkies. Poor Max.

Mamie was yelling into the cordless phone about a short bus, a coal truck, and a hearse. I bet dispatch was loving that. Someone helped the coal truck driver out of the cab, and I ran down and gave him a towel because he was bleeding where his head snapped and hit the steering wheel. We almost got run over by a couple of other truckers who were trying to squeeze through before the cops closed the road, the funeral home people were trying to get Ragin' Rod resettled and back into the hearse, I could hear about twenty snotsuckers crying, fifty bikers cussing, and a partridge in a pear tree. It was a goddamn mess.

Percy was heaving his guts out beside the road, and wouldn't you know that's what started this whole thing. Seems that one of the Combs twins, either Elmer or Delmer, barfed up his egg and bacon breakfast on the way to the Exceptional Students Social Studies Fair. (I told ya those boys shared a brain cell.) He happened to be sitting on the front seat, and the smell was so bad Percy and the front half of the bus all started gagging, then a few more of the kids started puking, and Percy took matters into his own hands.

Mrs. Masters, who was old when I was in school, staggered off the bus as green as a gourd. Her face was pinched up like a walnut, and I guarantee she's seen more kids puke than an ER, so it must've been pretty bad. Mrs. Masters is on the opposite end of the spectrum from Midge, she's a giant. The woman must be pert near blind because her glasses are so thick they give her cow eyes, and she had a way of looking at you that made you feel like she was pressing her long, bony finger into the center of your chest, and that's even before she started talking. But I'll tell ya this, she loves the special kids. Although some of them were still crying, they all filed out of the bus behind her and sat down on the edge of the road like she told them to.

"Percy?"

Percy spat a few times, wiped his nose on his hand, then stood up and faced Mrs. Masters.

"YOU'RE FIRED!"

"You cain't fire me!"

"It's not a matter of whether I can or can't, I am anyway! You almost killed us, twice! First by *flipping a U-E* in Morton's curve when I asked you to bring us back to the school, and then by that *insane, asinine display of abominable ignorance in passing a funeral procession and almost hitting head-on with a coal truck!* I will see to it or I'll see myself *out* the door. Virgie, I assume you've contacted the proper authorities?"

It took me a second to realize she was talking to me and to remember what "proper authorities" were. That's another thing about Mrs. Masters, she likes those hundred dollar words. I told her Mamie had called the cops. She seemed satisfied and walked over to the children and bent down and talked to each one. None of them looked hurt, unless you count being covered with puke.

The amazing thing is nobody died, and no one really got hurt that bad, and, if you can believe it, Ragin' Rod got his ass in the ground before noon. Midge marched up to Trooper Manny and demanded that they be allowed to go on to the cemetery because Rod had told her if he couldn't be put in the ground before noon not to bother and just wait until the next day.

"I ain't payin' for an extra night of chillin', are ya following me?" Midge said. Even though Max told her it wouldn't cost her any extra to house Rod overnight again, Trooper Manny let them go after Max told him he would file a statement later that day. You just don't tell Midge no.

As for Percy, he lost his job all right, problem is, so did Mrs. Masters. Well, they can say she took retirement, but the real reason she lost her job is because she's old school. She probably still carried a wooden ruler up her sleeve to snap on students' behinds when they made fun of the special kids, and from the looks of her, she was still wearing the same suits she wore when I was there, all gapped open in the front to make room for her quadraboobs. That's what we called her in school because she always wore her bras too tight, and it made her look like she had two extra boobs. Now I have a set of boobs that need their own seat in the car. That's what I get. Karma, she's a booby bitch.

Ditman was born with one eye that looked toward the dirt in his nostrils. Worms wiggled in his mouth and chiggers burrowed in the soles of his feet. He wore mittens for years to keep him from scratching the tracks of spiders and cockroaches that raced over his skin and the lice that fed at the edge of his scalp. As he got older, he shuffled his feet to cure the chiggers, but it stirred grasshoppers that jumped on his legs, and there were pitted scars where he picked and picked and picked at invisible bites.

His grandfather, Hiram, had tried to suffocate him in his third month. Ditman had been inconsolable with the spiders and cockroaches running rife and the chiggers and the lice, and his little hands covered with mittens so he couldn't scratch. Oh, the misery. He had screamed and screamed, hands flailing, pausing only long enough to draw another breath. No amount of bouncing, patting or pacing could cure the bugs, so he screamed until Hiram couldn't take it any longer and covered his mouth and pinched his nose.

"It's for the best," Hiram said, as he fought off his wife's clawed hands, his heart immune to her pleas to God. When Ditman laid still and blue, Hiram walked away, and Maggie had snatched him up and breathed into his lungs. When he refused to come alive, in a rage, she beat his body on the top of the table. Ditman's little heart started beating, and he twisted up his mouth, hitched, and howled. Hiram's shoulders slumped.

The next time he tried to take the baby, Maggie had pressed their old .22 into his crotch and told him he would never touch the baby again or he'd wind up without a pecker or a brain, his choice. "That boy would never be right," Hiram said, and he wasn't

The pediatrician told Maggie again and again the effects of the crack her daughter had smoked while pregnant would not cause Ditman to try and scratch himself now. Yes, he may have trouble sleeping, startle easy, and have trouble bonding, but otherwise, over the years, he would be just like other kids. He changed Ditman's formula and sent them home. The doctor was wrong. Ditman wasn't a normal child that could shake the effects of crack, and it was made worse when his grandfather tried to kill him and his grandmother bashed his poor soft head against the table to save him. It was a terrible, terrible combination.

In addition to his constant shuffling and the tic that caused him to scratch holes in his skin that festered and oozed, Ditman also had a strange relationship with spiders. Perhaps it was due to the constant agony he endured, not only of the feeling of bugs crawling on him, but also the cruelty of rejection that led him to catch spiders and pull their legs off. He took great satisfaction in how they squirmed, and even greater pleasure in watching them die.

During the summer between his tenth and eleventh grade years, Ditman got a part-time job at King's, a local gas station and body shop. He swept up and helped illegally dump oil in large pits in the woods. Hiram put his hand out for twenty-five dollars a week for driving him there and picking him up, even though it was only half a mile. Hiram never did give that boy a break. It only took one time for Ditman to buy a used bicycle.

After that, even when he wasn't working, he was doing something other than shuffling. He spent a lot of time sitting across from Lighthouse Inn, which was nothing more than a bar with five apartments attached. It sat at the base of Crawford Mountain and for Ditman to get there he had to climb the opposite side of the mountain alongside the sputtering coal trucks, sucking in their diesel fumes and an almost indiscernible mist of coal dust.

It wasn't that he lacked the money for what he wanted. He, unlike so many of his classmates, wasn't interested in knocking on the back door and paying double for a twelve pack or a fifth of Mad Dog. His only interest was in the center apartment where a local whore had set up shop to feed her pill addiction. It's not as though Ditman is a stranger to sex, just not that kind of sex. He's never been with a woman, although he desires to know the difference between a woman and what he does with Hiram.

Every Sunday he goes to Sunday School with Maggie, but every Wednesday she goes to the womens' meeting, and every Wednesday is when Hiram decided to teach Ditman about being a man. It started after Ditman had to relieve himself while he was helping outside, and Hiram saw his penis was circumcised. It was something they had done in the hospital after the State took control and before his grandparents were notified. Ditman was innocent in the decision, and he had no idea at the age of six whether he should be offended by the missing foreskin.

"Only Yids cut off their pricks," Hiram said, "I'll fix that."

Ditman's innocence in his circumcision was equal to his innocence in his naming. Ditman wasn't supposed to be his name at all. It was supposed to be Travis, Travis Allan Ditman, but his mother didn't understand the form and had transposed his first and last names, and since she wasn't married, she wasn't even allowed to give him his father's last name unless the father signed a form. The nurses wondered if she even did know for sure who the father was. So they changed Ditman's name to Ditman Allan Belcher. The belching titman, as he would be known among his more cruel classmates. The more intelligent of them didn't bother him. One of his cousins, a certain Flynn Mullins, once saw his good eye shift and narrow – the snake eye.

"He's got evil in him," she told her kin, and they left him alone as well. Flynn wasn't the only one who recognized the twisted essence of him that grew year after year. Maggie had on more than one occasion happened across Ditman as he tortured spiders, or seen the aftermath of a killing spree.

"Ditman, honey," she would say, and then say no more.

Ditman wasn't smart, but he wasn't mentally handicapped either. He had several learning disabilities, but the most remarkable of his deficits was the length of time it took him to discern right from wrong, which is why Hiram got by with what he did for so long.

The first Wednesday after Hiram saw his circumcised penis, he took Ditman to the tool shed on the edge of the property and told him to drop his pants. Hiram jerked Ditman's underwear down, then his own.

"You see this, boy? This is what a man's pecker looks like, not that little mushroom you have there."

Ditman stared at Hiram's penis, which to him looked like a larger, hairier version of the pigs in a blanket Grandma Maggie made on Saturday afternoons. He wasn't sure he wanted to look like Grandpa Hiram. The coarse gray hair that sprung around his penis looked like a winter-bleached thorn thicket. Then Hiram reached out and pulled down on Ditman's penis, hard, hard enough to make him wince, but it did make his penis look like a pig in a blanket. When Hiram stroked it a few more times, it started to feel good, and Ditman's little penis stiffened.

"Now, you have to do it to me."

Little Ditman was standing there with his underwear around his ankles alone and misunderstanding the right and wrong of this, scabs like polka-dots all over his body – legs, arms, the puffy little boy belly that his shirt couldn't cover, his neck, and his face with the one eye that turned inward. This shed is where Ditman would perfect his ability to capture and torture spiders, where he would be exposed to penises and pornography, where he would lose one half of his virginity, and where he would realize the right and wrong of it.

But we're not there yet. We're still sitting across from Lighthouse Inn gathering our courage. It wouldn't be this time, but two times later that Ditman would cross the scarred, pock-marked two lane and knock on the door of number three. Cassie Lyons would answer, her eyes half-glazed over, her robe hanging open from the waist.

121

"You got money?"

"Yeah."

She swings the door open and waits, and Ditman waits on the other side of the threshold.

"Well? You coming? You're letting the flies in."

Ditman steps inside and again waits. Cassie turns to him.

"Well, what do you want?"

Ditman takes a magazine out of the back of his pants and hands it to her. It's folded back to a particular page. Cassie sees nothing out of the ordinary, just a girl riding a guy, the tip of his penis inside of her, her butt cheek pulled up in the perfect position for the shot. Easy money.

"Okay, fifty bucks." A girl can always try, most of the time she charged twenty, then up from there, but he's green.

Ditman turns his back and counts out the fifty and hands it to her. She takes it then goes into the bathroom, comes out naked, lies back on the bed, and starts fingering herself, "I like to warm myself up, if you don't mind, while you get undressed." She's looking forward to getting him out of the way so she can call her dealer and pass out in peace. He has horrible scabs all over his body, but he isn't bad looking, and he has a nice dick. He stands at the foot of the bed, not doing anything, which Cassie finds odd. Most men lay their hands on themselves. She figures now that he's a virgin. Great.

"Come lay down with me."

"Ain't you gonna suck it?" he asks.

"That's an extra twenty."

He gives her another twenty. She tucks it under the edge of the mattress and takes his penis in her mouth. He puts his hand on the back of her head, which she hates, goddamn she hates that, but he seems all right, and she hopes it's just a bad habit. She feels him getting harder and starts to pull back to save him when his hand knots in her hair and he thrusts his penis further. Cassie struggles, pushing against his scaly thighs, but he only holds on tighter and pushes deeper. She gags and beats him with her fists while he orgasms. He lets her go, and she gags and spits.

"What the fuck are you *doing*?"

"That's the way it's done."

"No it's not you fucking dumbass! You pay extra for that shit!" She spits again, runs to the sink, and washes her mouth out.

"That's so fucking rude, you fucking idiot! God! Get the fuck out!"

"I paid you."

"You paid for a fuck and a little blow, not that!"

"I paid you," he says again, and this time there is an edge to his voice that penetrates her anger and the vestiges of the Oxycontin. It scares her. He stands between her and the door, his penis still carrying the half-hardness of youth. Cassie contemplates her options, and she figures it's best to move on with it and get him off and get him out.

"Right," she says, and then goes to the bed and gestures.

"You need to lay down."

He does and she strokes his penis until it is fully hard again, then spreads her lips and lowers herself onto him. His eyes, holy fuck, his eyes, one turns in, and the other, the other narrows and pulses like it's caught in a strobe light. Cassie bounces up and down, praying for him to orgasm, hoping he can get off as quick as he did before. She isn't disappointed, and she climbs off of him and goes to the bathroom. When she comes out, he's already dressed and sitting on the edge of the bed.

"Well, that's it. Time to go," she says.

"Do you do it in the ass?"

"Hell no! Ass fucking's for fags." That's what she says every time her johns bring it up.

Ditman stands, "I'm not a *fag*."

"I didn't say you were!"

"You said ass fucking's for fags, and I'm not a fag."

123

The edge to his voice is back, worse. This is the moment Cassie realizes just how alone she is.

"Okay, I think I would know, okay? I know you're not a fag. You're not, okay?"

Ditman sticks the magazine into the back of his pants and leaves. Cassie locks the door and throws the extra bolt, turns the lights out, and calls her dealer. A half hour later, she opens the door to a feeble knock, drugs and money pass hands, and Cassie sits at the little table, crushes two tablets, and snorts oblivion into her nose.

They say there are those that can see into the past, into the future, and beneath the shining veneers of falsehood, that even those with diminished capacities have some kind of gift. It isn't always true, but in Ditman's case it was. He did have the ability to see into the past, into the future, and beneath. How much he understood it, I can't say. I don't normally concern myself with such things. I only concern myself with the last breaths of mortals, so I am acquainted with Ditman, as I once stood at his shoulder, his soul in limbo. I lost. It happens a lot more frequently than you would imagine, cheating Death. I don't feel cheated, for I am not Death. I am the in-between.

We have many names and present many faces – angels, yamas, Valkyries, the Morrigan, Thoth, horses, dogs, and owls, among many, many others. How else would you come to the gate? Would you rather wander alone or would you prefer a companion who knows the way? Here's the secret I can tell, there's only one gate. What lies on the other side of it is the light, and what is within the light is "to each their own." There, feel better now?

Do not think me unfeeling, for I have seen the best and the worse of mankind throughout history. I have no power other than to comfort the dead in their transition. It's a small consolation for having to hover over the shoulder of Death as the soul wrestles with the body. It can be quite boring also. Often Death and I sit in the same room, waiting, shifting around, checking our cosmic watches. It's very complicated sometimes. Lessons have to be learned, Karma has to come around, then the Creator has to give the sign, then Death, then me. Most of the time, though, it's instant, blink of an eye, death's in and out, I'm in and out, it's done.

Then you have the Ditmans of the world, who are determined to make our jobs that much more difficult. I get all of my information from Death, because Death is omnipotent. Death is as much a part of the air you breathe as Life is. I always show up on the ass end of things, out of the loop, but Ditman was kind enough to give us time to catch up. When you're called in and Karma is sitting in the corner, you know it may be a while.

Ditman dawdled all day. Hiram smacked him in the back of the head several times to bring him back around to breaking up the clods of dirt left behind by the tiller. It was Wednesday, and the day after Ditman's evening with Cassie. He had had another dream the night before, the one where Hiram is smothering him and he's briefly lifted out of his body, and he wakes up gasping for air, his head hurting from the flogging it received on the kitchen table. He's known this for a while. Yesterday he proved he could be with a woman, he had seen that also, and he proved to himself that he wasn't a fag and that things are done different ways. That was the end. His visions and dreams, the knowing he had that he didn't understand, led the way, and even before he understood it, he started planning, because he saw that too.

"Come on, retard. Help me put this tiller up," Hiram said after Maggie had waved goodbye from the driveway. Ditman, obedient, dull Ditman, followed him. Ditman wasn't sure of what courage really meant or if he had any, but when he walked into the shed behind Hiram and picked up the paint can, it felt good in his hand.

Hiram awakened into an excruciating headache and a crushing feeling in his chest. He forced his eyes open in the dim light. He was confused by the knee on his chest, but when he tried to shove it off, he realized he's naked and his arms were spread and tied down to the legs of the old weight bench where he and Ditman. . . Ditman.

"What are you doing, boy?"

Ditman leaned harder on this chest and Hiram struggled, pulling at the ropes as Ditman pinched his nose and covered his mouth. Then Ditman stood up and Hiram sucked in a breath and coughed. Ditman grabbed his face.

"How's it feel, Grandpa? I know what you did, so how's it feel?"

"You fucking little imbecile, you let me go! You don't know anything!"

Ditman sat down beside him on a stool, his hands clasped in front of him.

"I know what you did," he said again, "And I know you never cared what it was like with the bugs, and I know I ain't a fag. You're the fag."

Ditman picked up an old pickle jar with holes punched in the lid. Inside were twenty-seven spiders, not your typical house spider with their teardrop bodies and spindly legs, but wolf spiders. Spring had been early and warm, and the wolf spiders had already emerged from their burrows. With their legs, some of them were the size of quarters. It made them easier to handle. A few did escape as Ditman dropped them onto Hiram's face. A few scuttled, then stopped, then scuttled, and did so enough that Ditman was able to allow them to scurry over Hiram's face more than once.

"This is what it feels like," Ditman intoned, over and over as Hiram jerked and twitched, but he was afraid to open his mouth for fear a spider would fall in, and Ditman knew that. That's why he clamped Hiram's nose shut with a clothespin and two roach clips, and as Hiram tried to breathe in through his nose, grunted and struggled, he had to open his mouth, and when he did, Ditman dropped the spider in. Hiram gagged and again did everything he could not to breathe in.

126

"That's what it feels like," Ditman said, and he kept dropping spiders in as Hiram's eyes teared and he gagged and strangled and strained and twisted his head from side to side and spiders ran everywhere. Hiram can see Ditman's pupil contracting and expanding, until it contracts and freezes. Then Ditman picked up a sawed off rake handle.

Karma was sitting in the corner smoking a cigarette, and she has this annoying habit of blowing smoke out of her nose and giggling at inappropriate moments, but that's what Karma does. It was no surprise that she was there considering what Ditman endured in his life, but that doesn't mean things don't get awkward, especially when it takes so long for Death to get the go ahead. It took a long time.

We did have double duty that evening. When Maggie returned from the womens' meeting, Ditman was sitting on the porch swing, still covered in blood. Disbelief is a good thing sometimes, it keeps the shock from killing you outright. To his credit, when Maggie asked where Hiram was, Ditman told her not to go to the shed.

"Don't go out there," he said, "He knows what it feels like now."

But whoever listens? When Maggie saw the carnage, her husband's ass in the air, bolstered on last year's lawn chair cushions, the rake handle sticking out of his rectum, the blood, and spiders, spiders everywhere, she backed away. There was no disbelief, only shock, and that's what got her.

Ditman hadn't seen that in his visions. He went to her and pounded her body against the earth and breathed air into her lungs, but Death had already come and gone, and her soul and I were halfway to the gate. He laid down with her, as she had done him so many times, and there they rested until late the next morning when the postal carrier noticed their bodies in the yard. Shock almost got him too, but he had enough sense to run back to his wrong-sided van and tear out for the next neighbors' house to call the police.

There are things that are done that can never be undone, things that are seen that can never be unseen, and they echo, they echo for years, for lifetimes, for generations. You don't want Karma sitting in your corner smoking a cigarette, just Death and I waiting for the signal to release your soul and carry you away.

Remember.

Karma

This here is a true story. When people hear it for the first time, they think I'm lyin', but that's because they like pretty things, and the truth is almost always ugly.

It started about five years ago over at Camp Smiley Trailer Park, and the reason everybody is smiling over there is because they're either drunk or stoned. Camp Smiley was also home to one of the biggest meth operations in the county, until Roger Fulmer got greedy and blew the entire bathroom right off the end of his doublewide, and this happened right after that at his brother Cal's place.

From what I understand everybody was having a high time boozing and smoking and among them was Wanetta Ramsey. Now, Wanetta had a disease nobody could remember how to pronounce but it paralyzed her throat so she couldn't swallow. Everybody called her Sissy and had since I can remember. Besides, who wants a name like Wanetta. Now, Sissy took everything through a feeding tube, including her booze, and if she turned sideways and stuck her tongue out she looked like a zipper, a homely one, with crooked teeth.

She'd been dating this sorry piece of shit named Kevin Harshbarger who was as mean as a copperhead and not quite as smart. Kevin was a "bragger." If you'd done anything, he'd done it and done it better. If you blacked your old lady's eye, well, he'd black both of Sissy's. That's the truth, I tell ya. I'd seen her after he got finished with her, just a rattling mass of bruises and bones.

About now you're probably feeling sorry for ole Sissy, but let me tell you what she did. Kevin was off doing God knows what the evening of Cal's party. Maybe they'd had a fight, I don't know, but what I do know is that Sissy got real friendly with a feller named Matt Strom. Matt was kind of new to town and had met Cal at the Rio D. while they were slinging back shots, playing darts and listening to drunk chicks trying to sing to the karaoke machine.

The Rio is a just a few steps above a hog trough. The wooden floor has lost its shine and the planks are just far enough apart that you can wedge in a high heel for leverage while you're breaking up a fight. We open at seven in the a.m., and every day Kurt Zetazelo and Frank Melville are waiting for me on the doorstep. Frank had told me once he'd never go to a bar that didn't have a wood floor. When I asked why, he said it was easier to mop up the blood. Lordy Jesus.

Anywho, seems Sissy and Matt had "sexual relations" in the bathroom there in Cal's trailer. I heard he said it was like fucking a sack of antlers. Course, everybody there knew it, and Sissy knew they knew, so, instead of doing the right thing and taking her beating from Kevin, she lied. She told Kevin she had been "assaulted." Now, I figure if you weigh it out, maybe she was afraid for her life. I can see that. But you never really know how far a lie will take you, until it's all over.

Kevin has a powerful mean heart about him, and probably the right thing to do would have been to call the police and report it, but that's just not how things are done around here. If somebody ain't dead or dying, don't bother. Instead, Kevin takes Sissy's brother, Randy, and his good buddy Bertram, to find Matt.

Now, Randy has huffed enough paint to kill all of his brain cells and some of yours, and at that time he'd probably had five or six DUIs. Needless to say, but I'll say it anyway, all the shine had done rubbed off of his penny. And Bertram, Lordy Jesus. Bertram worked down at the 24 Hour Adult Video Superstore off the four lane which sits directly next to the Savior's Hill Baptist Church. There's a sight. Bertram is one of those guys that creeps you out just by breathing in your direction. It didn't help matters that he always looked like he needed a shower and had one hand in his pocket. I heard rumors about blow up dolls and that sometimes he picked up extra shifts in the "adult entertainment booth," which is a fancy way of saying, "I know you thought it was a chick on the other side of that glory hole, but. . . "

These three peckerheads track Matt down to another bar, buy him a beer, and then offer to go out back and smoke a joint with him. I know I would have been concerned at this point because that's the redneck mating call. Once he follows them outside, they toss him into the back of Kevin's rusted out Buick and head out to the country. They ended up on the two lane bridge past Lower Falls near the turn hole.

They beat him good, really good, and then Kevin and the boys boosted him up and over the side of the bridge and into Coal River. Now, a few years before that some old lady had hit a deer at the end of that bridge and swore if there'd been a light there she wouldn't have. It was by that lone street light, way out in the country, that Kevin could still see Matt moving around down in the shallows.

Now, it could have ended here. Matt would have walked up to the road and maybe gotten a ride into our dinky ass town and called the police. Kevin and the boys would have been sent to county jail, plea bargained, and been out in ninety days. Instead, Kevin went down to the river and he held Matt under. He held that boy's head underwater until he drowned. That there is meanness, pure meanness.

Course, we all heard about it. It was big talk at the Rio D. for a while, then as things go, more things happen, you forget. Except one night Kevin got ripped and told me and my Momma and her boyfriend that he'd done it. Like I said, Kevin can't stand for anybody to be better than he is, but he's so full of shit his eyes are brown. I thought he was lyin'. Momma rolled her eyes and elbowed her boyfriend to stop asking questions and egging him on. That wasn't the only time I heard him talk about it, but I tried to ignore him. It gave me the creeps.

He may have gone on telling this story and we all may have nodded and thought, "He's full of shit" for a long time if it hadn't been for Randy and his DUI. Despite his numerous run-ins with the law, Randy still liked to get drunk and rattle around town in his red hatchback Cavalier. Every cop in three counties knew that car. If it was on the road, it was a given that whoever was driving it was gonna get pulled over, and this time it was Randy. A very drunk Randy, who told Patrolman Coffey that if he'd let him go he'd tell him who killed that boy out in Lower Falls.

They took Randy to the local police department and called in the sergeant, who also doubled as the detective, and Randy spilled his guts. Before you know it, police are crawling around down at the 24 Hour Adult Video Superstore, interrupting Bertram's latest fantasy fling and then come to the back door of the Rio D.

Didn't take long to figure out that for once in his life Kevin was telling the truth. What none of us could figure out was why he'd done it. In a community as small as ours, it was unusual not to know everybody's business before they did. Word spread quicker than a Baptist prayer chain. The Rio D. was packed that night.

Course cops are the biggest gossips I've ever known and it was only a matter of time before Sergeant Peterson told his third wife, who told her cousin, who told his sister, who told the entire congregation of Lower Falls Church of God why Kevin had done it. Which meant that right after church on that Sunday, my cousin, Thermy, called to let me know what Sissy had done.

I bet you're not feeling so sorry for Sissy now. I know I wasn't, not with cops crawling around all the time, scaring business away, and the worst, making me go to court.

When I walked in to testify, my knees were knocking. Kevin had sent a message out to all of us he'd been bullshitting for years that he was going to kill each and every one of us for testifying against him, starting with Randy and Bertram and ending with me and Momma. That pissed me off. Say what you want to about me. Do what you want, but don't mess with my momma. Yeah, she's a little bit of a drunk, and a little bit of a whore, but I love her all the way down her little peroxide blond head to her dark roots. We had our bags packed in case Kevin got off, but he didn't. He got life.

Randy got off as part of his plea deal only to be sent to

prison later for another DUI or running drugs or something like that. Bertram got ten or fifteen years on his deal and I figure he'll be out soon and back at the 24 Hour Adult Video Superstore using all of his newly learned prison skills.

And that leaves our darling Sissy, the little liar who started this whole mess. I saw her obituary in the paper. It said she died after a short illness, which could mean anything from an infected hangnail to a spider bite, so I called Thermy to get the scoop.

I laughed, and Thermy got mad and hung up on me, and then called back and admitted that she laughed too, but she'd deny it if I ever told anybody. Then we got real serious, and I said, "Karma sure did bite her in the ass."

Thermy said, "It sure did. God forgive us for laughing, but I ain't never seen nothing like it, and probably won't ever again."

Like I said, Sissy couldn't swallow, and she died by drowning. . . in her own spit. Karma's a bitch now, y'all.

135

Jerry and Little Boy

In a little trailer up a holler beyond the end of the road lived a man named Jerry. Jerry could have been a cliché, a cliché mountain man with his home cut hair and his long white beard stained yellow around the mouth from cigarettes. One may anticipate a couple of mangy, hateful curs that lived under his rotting porch to come boiling out, snarling and snapping at trespassers, and perhaps that Jerry himself would sit on his rotting little porch with a gun slung over his lap or at least within arms' length. But none of those things were true. Jerry didn't own any curs or any other dogs, he shared his home with a cat named Little Boy.

Little Boy was a dashing black and white tom with big yellow eyes who left his pungent piss mark everywhere he went. He was fat and sleek from his diet of moles, field mice, and an occasional bird, and it was easy to see that Jerry favored giving Little Boy wet cat food because white garbage bags piled in the back of his truck bulged with the edges of flat tin cans. So much so that some wondered if both Jerry and Little Boy ate it.

This is not where Jerry and Little Boy had started. Jerry used to live on the main road in a little clapboard house with central air and heat, and what the locals called "city water," which was a misnomer in that there wasn't a city within miles, it was just to differentiate between well water and water that had been treated and could be shut off if you didn't pay the bill. The main road wasn't a highway or an interstate or even a street, it was just blacktop with yellow and white lines that in winter and spring became a dodge 'em course – dodge this pothole, dodge that pothole – and everyone laughed that you could never tell if anyone was driving drunk because everyone zigged and zagged.

In summer, the state road came through and dumped more asphalt in the holes, and you could see the layers of fixes, the original, now gray, blacktop, then a darker gray layer, and another darker gray layer, and the new fix. Then an overweight coal truck would come through and the new asphalt, just as the other layers had done, would bulge out on the edges and the pothole would start over. It didn't take long to figure out why everyone zigged, zagged, or, more often, drove straddling the yellow line.

Now I can tell you how Jerry came to be in the holler beyond the end of the road, but don't think this road was the one with any lines on it. This is a holler road without lanes or lines, just a lot of potholes and a wicked, deep ditch that hides among the weeds. This was further than the turn off to Hardscrabble Road, further than the yellow mine gate, and past Camp Two, but not before you go over Williams Mountain. It's pretty far back, which is why Jerry puts his garbage in his truck bed because "city trash" doesn't run out here, you have to take your own garbage to the county dump, and if you're like Jerry, some days he just didn't feel up to it.

Unlike everyone else in the vicinity who could claim a plethora of kin, Jerry had come from Bolt Mountain, his one sister had passed early, he had never married, and as far as he knew, he had no children. He had worked in the mines as a roof bolter. Let's go inside the mine, and I will show you what happened to Jerry.

You see, maybe some people have the idea that coal mining involves men and women crawling on their hands and knees with only a headlamp to light the way. You've seen that image before, right? That isn't entirely true anymore. They do have electricity in the mines. That image is of low coal, where you can't stand up, or you have to stoop when you walk. This is high coal, the ceiling may be six or seven feet, and that's why you need roof bolts. Coal isn't hard like granite, it's soft. You can break it apart with your hands. That's why men used to dig it with spades and shovels and pitch it into carts that were drawn by mules.

Jerry worked on a roof bolter crew. Maybe you're thinking now that a roof collapsed on Jerry, but that didn't happen. Perhaps that would have been better. The bolter was run by a long, thick electrical cord that was operated by a switch that sucked it up or let it out depending on the need. Sadly, the torque on that cord was too high, this cord as thick as a man's arm, and while you may believe that all coal mines are dry and dusty, this is not the case.

That day there was a layer of mud about six inches thick and beneath it lay the electrical cord, invisible to Jerry as he went about his duties in the way he had been trained. On a normal day with a normal bolter, I would not be telling this story. Instead of the cord winding slowly when the operator hit the button, the cord whipped, and despite the fact Jerry was standing where he should have been, the cord caught him below his right knee with such force it flipped him into the air. Had it not been for the six inches of mud, it may well have broken Jerry's back.

Imagine, if you will, what the whipping action of an electrical cord as thick as a man's arm will do to a man's leg. *Crushing, broken, external fixator, nerve damage,* should come to mind, if you are having trouble with that. In reality, the cord almost amputated Jerry's leg, and this is how Jerry lost everything.

I can see those of you screaming "Workers' Comp!" have never had to live on it. Stop that, please. A mortgage and utilities and a truck payment, for a very nice truck I may add, and a credit card or two, and the four-wheeler, and a small piece of property he was paying on that he hoped to retire to someday, all that went to shit. After weeks in the hospital and then at a rehab center because Jerry had no family, and really no one he could ask or even think to ask through the haze of pain and painkillers to take care of things for him, it was on the edge of too late and then it all fell over in a little heap. It was over and done and Jerry had nothing, or so it seemed.

He did have a little money in savings and his Workers' Comp check, and he bought a little truck for a couple hundred bucks, and a little trailer for a couple hundred bucks, and he heard that the coal company was leasing land dirt cheap up past Camp Two, and this is where he moved and where he met Little Boy.

There was a creek that flowed out of the holler, like every holler, and Jerry took a chunk of money that he couldn't afford and had a well sunk because, as you know, he was out past "city water," and Little Boy was one of four kittens born to a feral mother who drank from the creek near Jerry's place. Little Boy was the only one who lived and was too malnourished and dehydrated when Jerry found him to struggle as a feral cat should. Little Boy was black and a dingy shade of gray, from coal dust, and that was what hair he had, and what portion of hair he had was matted with flea shit and those little sticky burrs, the real little ones.

Jerry fed him water and milk from a dropper, and Little Boy would try to clasp the smooth tip with his little white claws, the same way he grasped Jerry's finger as Jerry fed him fingertip portions of cat food. It was little wonder then that Little Boy followed Jerry everywhere he went, and Jerry had no need for a dog because he had Little Boy.

In the middle of the night, when Jerry would wake with his nerves burning from his back to his shattered leg bad enough to make him cry, Little Boy would lie with him and put his paw on Jerry's face. Jerry pet him with hands trembling from pain and listened to Little Boy's purr as he waited for the painkillers to take effect, and even when they did sometimes it only reduced his pain to a gnawing constant throb. In winter, Little Boy settled on Jerry's blossoming gut brought about by little exercise and cheap, fatty foods, covered with a thick blanket against the cold seeping in through the thin windows, the uninsulated floor, and the wide gash under the front door that Jerry tried to quell with an even thinner towel.

In summer, a window air conditioner rattled night and day and dripped water into a puddle on the ground. Jerry sometimes felt better, and he and Little Boy would walk to the creek, and over time Jerry realized there weren't minnows or crawdads in the creek anymore, the well pump would burn up, corroded with brown and black gunk, and a rusty ring appeared in the toilet and the bathtub that he couldn't scrub out, and then the hot water tank went bad. As you know, Jerry didn't have a lot of money and fixing the pump had taken his meager savings, so for a while he heated water on the stove to wash in and it stained the bottom of his pot. Then he got another check and a new hot water tank.

Have you figured out yet that living on coal company property and drinking the water downstream from a mine may not be that healthy? Jerry didn't think so either, but what choice did he have? What choice did his neighbors have? Yes, he did have a neighbor. He could see their front porch from his front porch, and he and Jacquetta Barker Reynolds, that would be Hershel Barker's sister who grew up in the Peeling Paint House, would wave to each other and speak of the weather and a bit of gossip when they crossed paths.

Jackie Reynolds took a great interest in Jerry, although he wasn't aware of it. She knew his story, and she tried as best she could to look after him. Her husband, Steve, worked in the mines, and Jerry was a constant reminder of what could happen, which is why they had moved up the holler on the dirt cheap coal company property and into a cheap trailer they could pay off faster, and why they drove a used truck. Jackie had grown up poor, and that should tell you enough.

I will warn you that the end of our story is a sad one, and you may become angry with me for telling you the truth. No one likes the truth. I believe someone has told you this before. The truth is almost always ugly.

It begins first with Jerry, who has lived in the holler the longest. It begins as what he thought was a boil on the back of his neck, perhaps a large zit or an infected spider bite that wept a bit of pus and blood, then scabbed, then wept until he had to cover it with a band-aid because at times it drained enough that it made his shirt wet. The little Indian doctor he went to shook his head when he asked about it and prescribed Jerry a cream that was butt-ass expensive and didn't do anything.

In a few months, the boil type place had taken over the back of Jerry's neck, so much so Jerry now walked with his head down a bit. It was the size of a golf ball, then the size of a tangelo, and well on its way to the size of an orange when Jerry lost the feeling in his left leg, and one morning he awoke with a headache and blind in his left eye. I bet you're thinking that little Indian doctor didn't know what he was doing, but he did. The month after he prescribed the cream, his mouth disappeared in a thin line when he looked at Jerry's neck, and he sent Jerry for an MRI.

Since that time, Jerry has known he has a tumor in his spine, and three in his brain, the largest of them the size of a walnut that sits behind the optic nerve of his left eye, and the words that should come to mind now are *radiation, chemotherapy, shrinking, growing, inoperable, blindness, paralysis,* and *death.*

Jerry shakes his head though and declines their offers for radiation and chemotherapy. It won't change the outcome, and he is willing to live out what life he has as he is. So, Jerry is dying. Aside from the growth on the back of his neck, he loses weight, his skin pales, and his once magnificent white beard loses its fullness and breaks into scraggy pieces. Also evident, at least to Jerry one day, is that Little Boy is also sick. He's also lost weight, his coat poor, and when Jerry rubs him he can feel his spine, his hipbones, and tumors under his armpits, then on his belly. They lay in bed together, these dwindling souls, and Little Boy no longer flicks his tail, and one day when he looks at Jerry and puts his paw on his face, one eye is bulging, weeping, and won't close. Later he will spasm and seize and writhe on the floor for a few moments, then sit up, and shake his head again and again, as though he's trying to dislodge the tumors within him.

It doesn't take long. On the day Jerry has convinced himself to take Little Boy to the vet and ease his suffering forever, Little Boy puts his paw on Jerry's face, seizes in a most horrific way, meowing and growling, and dies. Turn away, dear reader, so you do not have to see the anguish. It is unbearable, I assure you. I assure you that you do not want to see this man, beaten in so many ways, gaunt and

141

brokenhearted, say good-bye to his most loyal friend. Don't listen to his sobs and his choking voice as he tells Little Boy what he has meant to him for so many years and how sorry he is that he couldn't save him and sorry that he wasn't stronger to ease his suffering sooner and sorry that he was so selfish, but he loved him so much. Love gets in the way, doesn't it, of doing the right thing sometimes?

This is the end for Jerry, too. He wraps Little Boy in the thin towel he uses in the gash under the door, and he holds him in his arms like a baby, then sits in his easy chair where they spent many, many hours together, and as the doctor said might happen, one of those tumors bulges and Jerry has a stroke, and when Jackie Reynolds comes to check on Jerry, this is how she finds them. Jerry's head is tipped back, his eyes half-closed, and Little Boy has slipped deeper into the crook of his limp arm.

Jerry's cancer alarmed her, but this, this scares the sin out of her. Not that Jackie is a sinful woman, I don't want you to think that, but Jerry isn't the only one who is sick, and while she doesn't know it yet, she's sick too. Over half of the residents of this holler will die of cancer within five years. She is one of them. They all knew it was the water. The runoff from the mines leached into the water table and into their wells. It's poison, but that's a secret.

You see, when this started happening, people got scared, and they started asking questions and asking for water samples, and they started making phone calls. It wasn't long until word of this *uprising* reached the ears of the wrong person, and suddenly the mine above the holler where all of this took place shut down, then another, and another. Neighbors fought. People who had known one another for all of their lives refused to speak. The media spewed warnings of more layoffs, and people became more fearful and more uncomfortable until those among them that dared to rise up were quashed. Divide, conquer, control.

I'll tell you last where Jerry is buried. It's in the hill section of the closest local cemetery. His grave is very plain.

There isn't a gravestone, only a thin aluminum plate that states his name, the date of his birth, and the date of his death, and only one person, Jackie Reynolds, knew that on the night of his burial a hole was dug in the fresh earth of his grave, and within lies the body of Little Boy, and only she knew, and will ever know, because she's the one who did it.

King Oxy

A worthless person, a wicked man, goes about with crooked speech, winks with his eyes, signals with his feet, points with his finger, with perverted heart devises evil, continually sowing discord; therefore calamity will come upon him suddenly; in a moment he will be broken beyond healing. –
Proverbs 6:12-15

Anna sits with her head in her hands and, in the safety of this artificial darkness, she chews her lip. Overdue utilities bills and nasty letters from her landlord and the local *Buy Here! Pay Here! Everyone Approved!* car lot lay on the table. They quiver in the draft from the small window air conditioner that can never keep up with the brilliant, burning sun. Anna keeps the air conditioner turned up so it doesn't kick on as much, and the box fan with part of its grill missing sits silent. The more shit runs, the more the bill will be. Her son, three month old Noah, lies on his belly on a thin cotton blanket clothed in a diaper. Anna knows she's not supposed to let him, but he won't fall asleep on his back, he won't sleep on his back at all, and she is too tired to fight him any longer.

Her pregnancy had taken it out of her, her energy and her money. She qualifies for WIC and a little extra check, but the waiting list for housing assistance is seven years. Seven fucking years for a place in the HUD apartments. She asked her landlord, Ernie, if he would try to get on the HUD list. He flicked his cigarette at her.

"Hell no, then I'd have to fix these places up. Fuck that. Can't pay? Get out."

Anna doesn't have the money to go anywhere else. Camp Smiley is as cheap as they come. Her full-time job at the dingy little gas station dropped to part-time, they hadn't coughed up a dime when she took maternity leave, and anything she claims the State takes out of her assistance check while they chase her ex-boyfriend for child support. Good fucking luck. She still owes on the piece of shit car she needs

144

to get to work that sucks up more money than it's worth, and she's already exhausted the good graces of utility assistance as well. There isn't a place she hasn't applied for a better job, a full-time job, at least in the radius she feels her car could make it every day. She could have gotten on sitting with old people, but they wanted her to work midnights. Her sitter doesn't keep kids overnight and it makes Anna uncomfortable anyway.

When Anna told her mother she was pregnant, Loretta pointed her cigarette at her, and said, "Don't expect me to take care of it. You have 'em, you raise 'em." So Anna is reluctant to ask for help, plus she lives too far away to make it convenient. Her older sister, Virgie, works odd shifts at a bar, her younger sister, Sugar Ray, has two little ones of her own and works part-time with her husband at the funeral home, and Vickie, well Anna wouldn't trust her to watch a dog. Her cousin, Flynn, offered to help, but again, she lives too far away, or so Anna likes to say, but it is her pride, not distance that leads her to reject Flynn's offer. Anna was raised to believe if she worked hard everything would be okay. It is not okay.

When Anna gets home from work the next day, she had been let go early, which pissed her off because it would make her check short, there is another note from Ernie. She grabs the note and hitches Noah onto her shoulder a little higher, making sure to cover his head against the sun that beats on the back of her neck. She crumples the note and looks around at the rows of trailers in various stages of dilapidation. Ernie doesn't allow anyone to move a trailer into the trailer park, he owns all of the trailers, and he doesn't care much what you do to them. There isn't much else could be done to most of them, although, he was pretty pissed when Roger Fulmer blew his bathroom up making meth. The county came and condemned the whole site. He lost the trailer and the lot, at least until an appropriate waiting period was followed, and the white county truck stopped making passes

145

on the hill, then Ernie moved in another trailer. Camp Smiley sits on a hollowed out section of mountain that is above the flood plain. It doesn't matter if the holler floods and you can't get home or get out, it only matters that Ernie doesn't see his investment rolling down the creek. No way in, no way out. Or is there?

After nursing Noah and making a peanut butter sandwich, Anna goes next door. Her neighbor, Rhonda, always has a pile of garbage on the porch waiting to go the dump and three or four kids running around in various stages of nakedness.

Rhonda had been ahead of her a few years in school, and she was always snickering behind her hand and laughing too loud, always drawing attention to herself or making fun of someone. When Anna brought Noah home from the hospital, Rhonda came over to see them. She stood over them and took a good look at Noah, so much so Anna was prepared to kick her in her fat belly if she didn't back off.

"He looks pretty normal. That's a shame. If they're retarded, you can get a check for 'em."

Anna wondered if the little boy holding her hand understood, or would ever understand what Rhonda had said. He has Fetal Alcohol Syndrome and wears it all over his face. It could have been his picture on the wall of her obstetrician's office. And what parent let their flesh and blood become a poster child? Maybe that's how Rhonda made more money, maybe she loaned out her foster kids as a warning to other parents.

It makes Anna sick. She hadn't liked Rhonda then, and she sure as fuck doesn't like her now, but, Rhonda has something she needs.

Rhonda answers the door with a child on her hip. It's a different little boy. This one is wearing a pair of underwear that are too small, there's a hole that has started in the seam of the faded green waistband, the superhero no longer visible on

146

the thin material stretched across his bottom.

"Oh, hey, Anna."

"Hey, uh, can I get the name of that doctor you go to? I tripped over the, uh, I tripped and twisted my back."

Rhonda picks her teeth, sucks her finger, and chews.

"Sure."

Anna stands on the threshold, patting Noah's back, his soft baby smell soothing her nerves, bolstering her resolve. She hears a deeper voice, must be Rhonda's husband, and Rhonda comes back with a card. It is crisp and clean, as though kept in stack, and that's exactly where Rhonda keeps them, in a stack. She flips the card out, and when Anna tries to take it, Rhonda resists.

"You just make sure he knows that I sent ya, and if he asks if you're nervous, say yes."

Rhonda's eyes are hard, her voice husky.

"I will."

Rhonda releases the card.

"Don't forget."

Anna dials the number. When the receptionist answers, Anna says she needs to make an appointment.

"Do you have insurance?"

"I have a medical card."

"I have an opening Thursday morning at eight o'clock."

They always have an opening at eight o'clock. That's when new patients with medical cards are seen, every weekday morning at eight o'clock.

"And who referred you here?"

The doctor hasn't looked at her since he came in the room. He's foreign, but Anna has no idea where he's from. Everyone calls him Dr. G. Maybe it's the Philippines or Pakistan or Syria or the fucking North Pole. When Anna tells him, he nods his head, smiles a little, and asks why she's there. She tells him. He makes notes, turns, and hands her a prescription. Oxycontin – 20 mg. Twice a day. No refill. Anna does the math.

"Are you nervous? Having trouble sleeping?"

"Yes."

Scribble, rip, 2 mg. Xanax twice a day or as needed. No refill. She makes an appointment for the next month. She's still shaking when she gets in the car. She shakes all the way to the pharmacy. She shakes until the pharmacist hands her the bag. It's a pharmacy she never uses on the other side of the county.

"Whadya get?"

Anna hands Rhonda the bag.

"Nice. Twenty each for the Oxys, five each for the Zannies," Rhonda popped the lid on the Xanax and took one, "For later. I know some people probably be needing some right now. Save one for Ernie. He might knock a little off the rent."

By six o'clock all of the pills are gone, Ernie's been paid, minus fifty dollars, plus a pill. The next day Anna pays her car payment, gets her utilities to more reasonable sums, buys two packs of diapers, a pack of wipes, washing detergent, fabric softener, and a jar of jelly. WIC doesn't pay for jelly, and she's tired of dry peanut butter sandwiches.

Anna knows it's just a band-aid for her larger problem, and all she wants is to break even. She's close to being caught up. If her hours stay the same maybe she can swing it, until she wakes up one morning, her hair drenched with sweat because the air conditioner has shit the bed, her car needs new tires, and Noah needs diapers and clothes. Anna is frugal, though. She does buy a new air conditioner, the first thing she's ever had that someone hasn't owned before, but her tires are used, and she drives an hour away to pick up hand-me-downs from one of her cousins.

Anna is afraid she's getting herself into something she won't be able to get out of. She's already broken one promise to herself, and that is she's gone back to Dr. G. sooner than she should have and complained about extra pain so he will give her a new prescription in a higher dose so she can make more money. She fills the prescriptions at a revolving set of pharmacies, and some day they will start tracking these prescriptions, but for now, everyone is blissfully ignorant, except the police and social workers, who are seeing more and more pill heads.

In her favor, Anna doesn't take any of the drugs prescribed to her. She's still nursing and pumping, although some days the stress of lying and the trips to the pharmacy and the fear, it makes her wish she could just pop one of those Zannies and disappear in a haze, but she's afraid of that too. Car doors slamming make her jump. She spends an inordinate amount of time stationed in the trailer so she can see out of the windows, especially the large window at the front of the trailer where she can see the road going up the hill. She's sure someone's going to turn and the police will come knocking.

In anticipation of this happening, her trailer is as clean as an old trailer can be. Noah is also clean and smells good, his vaccinations are up to date, his every need fulfilled. At night, she paces the length of the trailer, his still tiny head sprouting new golden curls snuggled into her neck, and it isn't so much that he needs her to sleep, but she needs him to stay calm. Losing him is her greatest fear. Anna kisses his head and rubs her cheek over the moist spot. She settles down on the sagging couch and picks up a pamphlet she snagged when she was at the store. It's for the vo-tech school, but it's also an hour away. She would have to move, which wouldn't be a bad thing.

The next day Anna calls her case worker and asks about going to school. She can get money, more money, and grants, but she knows she can't do it unless she moves. Her car will never make a two hour round trip every day, and if some of the classes are at night, she doesn't have anyone to take care of Noah, but, maybe she can.

Winter settles in and Anna closes the vents to the back of the trailer and hangs a thick blanket between the living room and the hallway to contain the heat, which she turns down to a horribly cold level. She prays the old furnace holds out. She and Noah snuggle under a blanket on the couch. They don't go anywhere other than work, the doctor, pharmacies, and the store. Anna goes back to dry peanut butter sandwiches.

Rhonda is pregnant. She found out right after Anna knocked on her door that day in the summer, and she's thrilled. She and her husband, Dave, have been trying for a long time. Truth be told, Rhonda's been trying since she was sixteen. She spends the first three months with her head hung over the toilet bowl and loses twenty-five pounds. She's meticulous about what she eats, and she makes Dave smoke on the porch. Almost all of his activities take place on the porch. He's a dealer too, but he's also a user, and that makes him susceptible to making bad deals.

Rhonda's a different person. She doesn't have as much patience with Dave's addiction or his dealing. She's much more concerned now that they're having their own baby. The visits from the social workers have calmed quite a bit. They have their hands full with meth houses full of rotten trash, dog feces, and drug addicted babies.

Still, she makes Dave go to the dump more often, and she nags at him to give up the pills because the mines are catching on and starting to piss test everyone. He blows every dime he makes up his nose, and sometimes into his veins, and Rhonda is ready to leave the hill and have a pretty little house. She is tired of living off the checks for the foster kids. She's ready to give them up all together.

Rhonda has turned into a mama bear, something she has never felt before. Despite the fact she has had two of the three children in her care since they were babies, she believes she won't or can't ever love her foster kids like she loves the one she is carrying. This bothers her more than she will ever be able to admit. She never thought she was that kind of person.

Come to find out, she isn't that kind of person. When Dave has a dirty piss and he loses his job, it isn't long before word reaches a social worker. When they come unannounced to pack up the three little boys, Rhonda asks if she puts Dave out if she can keep them. The answer is no.

Anna watches all of this from behind the kitchen curtain that overlooks Rhonda's porch. She doesn't touch the curtain. She stands at an odd angle so she can see out through the natural part, and she holds her hand over her mouth, not only to force her breath down so there is no chance of the curtain moving, but also because she is afraid and sad. The boys cry because Mommy cries. They have a symbiotic relationship with her, and when she feels fear, they feel fear. They don't understand. Anna can see their white teeth and the fleshy gums where their molars haven't started moving yet. She wants to wipe away their tears and drool and confusion. *Goddamn.*

These are the kinds of things that cause the web of deceit to collapse. When people start losing things - their jobs, their kids, their freedom, they start squealing on each other, anything to make themselves feel better about what has been taken from them instead of realizing it is no one's fault but their own.

Anna isn't any better. She knows she would sing, loud, if she had to make a choice between Dr. G. and Noah. After the car doors slam and the social worker drives away, Rhonda stands on the porch with her hands over her face, her body shaking, and Anna goes out to be with her.

She convinces Rhonda to go inside, lie down on her side, and sip water through a fat straw. Anna assumes Dave is hiding in the back.

"You'll dehydrate," Anna tells her. She knows because she had had her own breakdown during her pregnancy, and she cried enough to dehydrate herself which put her in the hospital for a dose of intravenous fluids. Anna vowed to never cry that much over a man again.

"I'm so sorry, Rhonda."

151

"Do you think they'll take my baby when she's born?"

"Of course not, you're clean. They send babies home with alcoholic daddies all the time. I don't see why Dave would be any different. Besides, if you have to, kick him out."

Anna says the last part in a soft, off-hand manner because she still doesn't know where Dave is, and she doesn't want him to hear her encouraging his wife to kick him to the curb.

"You don't have anything here do you, I mean, if the police show up?"

"Hell no, he does too much of it to keep any."

"Okay, then, you're fine." Right? They were all fine, weren't they?

Anna *is* fine. She lays low, skips her monthly visit to Dr. G. and parks her car on the other side of the trailer park so her regulars will think she isn't home. It's quiet anyway. Everyone knows what happened and no one wants to get caught. It doesn't last long. It never does.

The first hint of trouble is the first time Anna sees a new truck on the hill, a massive red beast with roll bars and a black grille guard. It roars as it comes up the hill, enough that Anna stands at the kitchen window and watches as Dave trots out and speaks to the driver. He has curly white hair, a full, well-trimmed beard, and a pug nose. Bill Mullins. He has a reputation for having a hand in just about everything illegal – moonshining, drug dealing, and copper theft. He is also her uncle, and he has a whole posse of thugs who do things for him, because, as her mother says, he is so lazy he won't hit a lick at a snake. It shows in the amount of bulk she sees from the window.

True, Bill Mullins isn't given to any type of fast movement, or movement at all, but to believe he is benign is a mistake. It must be serious if Bill himself is paying a visit. Anna watches Bill point his finger in Dave's face. Dave nods vigorously, and when Bill looks around and up toward her window, she moves back a little. There is no way she wants involved in this, not even a little.

A little later there's a tap on her door. It's Rhonda.

"Look, I know you don't have a lot, but I'm asking as a friend if you could maybe float us a loan. I can't be going in and getting prescriptions, and Dave, well, he's afraid because, you know, but we have to have it. You know, you can get more drugs."

Anna knows how to get more drugs. You went to a different doctor that everyone knows is scamming Medicaid, and you make your rounds of pharmacies. The more doctors you see and the more pharmacies you hit, the more you can sell. Some people have started crossing over into Kentucky for doctors and pharmacies, anything to hide the scam, the selling, and the addiction.

"I'm due for a doctor visit," Anna says. She hates giving it up, but she can tell Rhonda is afraid, and Anna is afraid for her.

"Try to get forties or fifties, okay?"

"Damn, Rhonda, how much do you need? You know I don't sell the high migs. That's big time."

A sweat breaks out on Rhonda's forehead, despite the fact it is uncomfortably cool in the trailer. March came roaring in like Bill Mullins and laid a layer of snow that refuses to melt.

"We need a lot."

Jesus.

The next day as Anna returns from the doctor's office, she sees Dave carrying their television to a car she doesn't recognize and money is exchanged. By nine o'clock, she has eighteen hundred dollars, her largest take so far. She didn't push for thirties, and definitely not forties, but she did push for an extra thirty pills.

She has heard things about Dr. G., and she doesn't want to get on his bad side. She isn't addicted, and most times she holds to the strict monthly visit for twenties which she feels keeps her under the radar. She doesn't badger him, except the one time, for higher doses and extra pills, and unlike the addicts, she isn't going to bend over the mossy green exam table with its cheap thin paper and let him fuck her for the script. That's for the tweakers in the waiting room. He scams his fifty-five dollars from the state, and she scams addicts for money and eats dry peanut butter sandwiches.

Anna's benevolence only goes so far, though. She is scared for Rhonda so she gives her the eighteen hundred, but not a dime more from the stash of dog-eared twenties she keeps hidden in the ceiling above the loose light fixture in Noah's closet. She doesn't buy a new car, a fancy TV, or a four-wheeler like so many of the other dealers without jobs that broadcast their profession by the toys they buy. She works a job, she sells drugs, she keeps her head down, and she stays poor.

Rhonda takes the money with a sigh.

"I got thirty extra pills, but only twenties."

"I 'preciate it, Anna. I'll make sure you get it back, just as soon as things calm down around here."

"Do you have enough?"

"No, we ain't gonna have it, but we got quite a bit, so, it'll be okay. We'll just, you know, work it out. You're a good person, Anna," Rhonda says as she turns away, "You're a good person."

Anna listens for the red truck to rumble up the hill. When she gets a drink of water, she sees the curtains are drawn and only a single light burns in the living room next door. She nurses Noah to sleep and listens to the radio, rereading a book she's read a dozen times before. She wishes she had a TV, something to distract her. Headlights illuminate her window, but she is sleepy and doesn't bother to get up because she doesn't hear what she's listening for. Instead, she curls up under a blanket and falls asleep. The sounds from next door, the ones she has been waiting on, go on without her.

Bill Mullins likes to make an entrance, except when it

goes down. Then he is nowhere to be seen, except miles away in a very public place drinking beer with one of his son's. Two of his other sons drive to Rhonda's trailer to collect. One of them is Ricky Belcher, one of Bill's four illegitimate children. Like his sister, Rose, he grew up believing Floyd Belcher was his dad, until Floyd died after a reaction to a snakebite while handling snakes, and Bill became much more of an influence in their lives.

As ruthless as Bill is about making money, Ricky's blood lust has been known to give Bill pause. Ricky's not afraid to pistol whip an old man for his ginseng or a young girl over an ounce of pot. Something else happened to that young girl, much more than a pistol whipping, but no one speaks of it. Bill's learned to keep Ricky contained because he has no conscience, and overkill only draws more attention to them, something Bill doesn't want. That's why Ricky isn't supposed to be at Rhonda's, but one his other brothers couldn't be there so Ricky said he would go, and no one argues with Ricky.

Ricky and his youngest brother, Danny, pull up in front of Rhonda's and cut the engine. It's late and not many lights are on. Dave waits for them on the couch. Rhonda sits on the edge of the bed in the back bedroom wringing her hands and praying because they don't have enough money to cover Dave's drug debt, and she wonders how bad they're going to beat him. She hears the door open and voices, raising voices, and footsteps. The door to the bedroom flies open, and Ricky is a dark shadow in the doorway.

"You hidin', huh? Get the fuck out here!"

"She ain't got nothin' to do with it, Ricky! It's my fault."

"Yeah, it's your fucking fault," Ricky says, and that's when Rhonda notices he has a gun.

"My God, my God, my God," she whispers as he pushes her through the hallway to the living room.

"Shit, Ricky, what the fuck, man?" Danny says.

Ricky doesn't answer, instead he turns his attention to Rhonda and Dave. Rhonda trembles and cradles the womb where her daughter kicks against the adrenaline influx, fight or flight. Dave stands in front of her, his arms outstretched in supplication, his hands shaking.

"Look, look, look, I gave you almost three thousand dollars."

He's just trying to scare us, Dave thinks, he's just trying to scare us, he's just trying to scare us.

"You owe over five grand, fuckwad."

"I know, I know, and we just need a little more time to raise the rest. We have people helping us, we just need a little bit more time."

"Times UP! Get down, get down on your knees!" Ricky waves the gun at them. Dave and Rhonda stare at him.

"Ricky, come on," Danny says.

"If you don't shut up, you little peckerhead, I'm gonna kill you too. I said to get down," Ricky grabs a hold of Dave and shoves him toward the ground, "on your fucking knees!"

Dave kneels, his hands still outstretched, thinking only *I'm gonna kill you too, I'm gonna kill you too.*

"Look, look, just, okay, it's my fault, okay? Rhonda, she don't have anything to do with this. She won't say nothin', will you babe? She'll be quiet, okay? Okay, man, she's pregnant, she won't say nothin'. You won't say nothin', will you babe?"

Rhonda shakes her head, in shock, in fear, fear that runs down her leg as her bladder lets go, and the smell rises and mixes with the pungent body odor of terror, and the little girl within her struggles as Ricky grabs her wrist and twists it. Rhonda cries out as he pushes her down beside her husband, and she finds her voice.

"Oh God, oh please, please, please, no."

The rush of power intoxicates Ricky, and he turns the gun to Rhonda's temple first.

"Ricky, man, come on! Stop this shit!" Danny yells.

"Please, please, no, dear God, please," and he shoots

156

her, and before Dave can beg, he shoots him as well. Danny stares at him, shocked and sick.

"Oh my God, Ricky! What the fuck! What the fuck!"

Ricky raises the gun and points it at Danny's head.

"Shut up ya little pussy. Shut the fuck up!"

"Ricky, we weren't, oh fuck, man, you just killed. . ."

"Shut up! I'll fuckin' kill ya if ya don't shut the fuck up. Let's go." Ricky grabs Danny by the front of his coat and shoves him toward the door.

Wake up, a voice whispers. Anna gasps and wakes.

Pop!

The cry of a newborn erupts from thin air and dissipates.

Pop!

Disoriented, she wonders if it was a dream. She hears muffled voices, and she gets up and goes to the window. She sees two men come out of the trailer. One shoves the other in front of him. They get into a dark pick-up and drive away. The living room light is still on at Rhonda's.

Anna slips her feet into her tennis shoes without bothering to tie them, goes outside and around the trailer. The ground is slick and slushy, and she walks sideways down the bank to keep from sliding. As she walks up the three steps to their front door, she sees something. It's a roll of bills bound with a rubber band. Confused, she picks it up and knocks on the door. She doesn't hear anything. She knocks again.

"Hey, Rhonda, it's Anna." Nothing. She knocks again.

"Dave! Rhonda!" Would they have left? How? Their car is still in the driveway. She turns the knobs and pushes the door forward.

"Hey, guys," she says and sticks her head inside. Rhonda lies almost face down, her body turned a little as her weight shifted over her pregnant body. Her mouth is open, but her eyelids sag near closed. The brilliant red blood has already begun to coagulate, and the smell permeates the room.

"Oh my God!"

Anna clenches her fists and brings them to her face.

"Oh God, oh God, oh God," she whimpers. Somewhere, a door slams, and Anna jerks and runs. She slips going up the bank, her knees sinking into the mud, and she claws her way up. Her hands are muddy, she can't get her front door open, then it's open, and her slush clogged shoes slide on the linoleum in the kitchen and she goes down, hitting her head on the floor. She rolls over, pushes herself up, and grabs the phone. It takes three tries for the dispatcher to understand.

"My neighbors, someone shot my neighbors."

Anna runs to the bedroom. Noah is lying on his stomach, his hands tucked up to his chin, his butt pushed in the air. She lays her hand on his back and absorbs his life – warmth, the slight rise and fall of breath. When she moves her hand, it leaves a muddy imprint. She staggers down the narrow hallway, the adrenaline seeping away, leaving exhaustion. She picks up the phone again.

Flynn dozes on the couch, one of her cats curled up in her lap, a fire burning in the fireplace when the phone rings. She makes the forty-five minute drive in thirty. Somewhere along the way blue lights and sirens pass her on double yellow lines, and she knows where they are going.

Anna sits at her tiny, two-person kitchen table, her hands, face, and clothes still muddy. Flynn wipes her with a dishcloth among the pulsing red, white, and blue lights, yellow crime scene tape, drab olive uniforms, and the taupe telephone that continues to ring with those who were listening to the scanner and are nib-shitting for gossip. Flynn unplugs it. Anna asks her more than once to check on Noah, and each time Flynn returns and reassures her that Noah is fine. Now Flynn stands at the kitchen window watching the activity at the trailer. She turns away as they remove Dave and Rhonda, their bodies shrouded in thick, black plastic.

Anna's great aunt, Bertie, had once told her that

Manny Stavrakis could make the biggest liar tell the truth and the biggest whore an honest woman.

"Don't believe all that Greek bullshit. He's part Gypsy. Don't look into his eyes, child, you'll be lost. You'll never be the same."

Many in the family try to disregard Aunt Bertie, but Anna isn't one of them. She has lost herself once already. Not only did Noah's father break her heart, he tried as hard as he could to break her spirit, the essence of her. He knocked her legs out from under her. He stepped on her throat to quiet her voice. He tried, but he did not break her.

So instead of looking into Manny's eyes, she looks instead at his hands. His skin is dark, olive, and his fingers taper into perfect crescent moon tips. He does not try to silence her. He writes her words on thick black lines that extend onto his hand and travel into the sleeve of his uniform. She wonders if the black lines are on his chest, if they crawl down his belly. She wonders if she can taste Gypsy in his sweat.

Manny's voice says he is in control, professional, strong, but within, his heart falls into disbelief, it breaks, it is hurt and angry, it cries out and flounders even as his steady hand writes words on thick black lines.

Calm, soothing, protective, (did Aunt Bertie mention his voice?) lulling Anna into answering his questions, dishonesty laced with honesty.

She saw two men and a dark pickup, but no, she didn't see their faces. She knew Dave had been fired from the mines, but no, she didn't know if they had problems with anyone. No, she hadn't seen anyone there earlier. No, she didn't know about any money problems. No, the TV wasn't stolen, someone bought it. Yes, she knew Dave did drugs, that's why he was fired, but no, she doesn't know who his dealer is, was.

His energy shifts back and forth, but she is studying his hands, not his eyes, so she does not know what secrets

159

they may reveal, until by accident, or perhaps curiosity, or a self-destructive inclination, she finds herself within his eyes, among the browns, golds, and greens (a silver shade of blue from a distant grandmother hides behind the pupil). She sees his true empathic nature.

And now he knows she is lying.

Bill sits in his recliner, his best friend, Big Mike Vealey, across from him. Big Mike is a Vietnam Veteran. He's got a bushy red beard shot through with gray, and he wears a floppy camouflage hat to cover the bald spot on the back of head. Big Mike doesn't walk, he lumbers, and he's a humorless man.

"I want you to take Ricky and go check out a new still site."

"Oh, yeah? Where 'bouts?"

"Maxine's Ridge, bunch of old mines and vent shafts up there. Be a shame if Ricky got lost in one."

Mike tips back in a kitchen chair, the bottom of the legs worn from this habit and Mike's considerable girth. He raises his eyebrows and gnaws on a piece of his mustache.

"Yeah?"

"Yeah," Bill says, and leans forward in his chair, "You got it, or do I need to do it myself?"

Mike shakes his head and spits a stream of tobacco juice in an old tin can, "Naw, I got it. What about Danny?"

"I'll take care of Danny."

Danny. Danny is a problem, but for a different reason. He came home that night sweating, shaking, crying, and bloody. Ricky had pulverized the side of his face with the gun. Ricky never could stand a pussy. That was the mess Bill had come home to, and he had helped strip Danny out of his clothes, down to his underwear, even his shoes, and he set it all on fire with gasoline in the fire barrel. He'd backhanded Ricky into the side of the shed.

"You dumb sonofabitch! What the fuck were you

160

thinkin'? You'll have every goddamn pig in the county linin' up outside!" It was more than that. It is two dead people, and one of them pregnant. It's sick, like Ricky. Sick like his cousin, Ditman, but Ditman had a reason for killing his grandfather. Ricky didn't need a reason. The boy wasn't right, and he never would be.

More than anything, Bill is a businessman. Sometimes he has to get rough, but even he has a limit. He walks softly, and he carries a big stick, and most often that's enough, and if it isn't, a good ass whipping helps to set things straight. He don't have much trouble, except for Ricky, and now Danny. Danny is soft and malleable. If the cops got a hold of him, he will sink them all.

Big Mike and Ricky take a ride into the woods. Ricky gets out of the truck, holds one nostril shut, and blows his nose onto the ground. Big Mike puts the gun to the back of Ricky's head and pulls the trigger. No talk, no warning. Big Mike takes him by the heels, drags him over to the ventilation shaft, and drops him long enough to adjust his britches and move the tin aside. Despite the cold, the smell of decomposition wafts to the surface.

"Goddamn." Big Mike lumbers to the truck, gets his flashlight, and when he shines the light inside, he sees another body, head down. He figures there's room for one more, and in goes Ricky. Big Mike wipes his hands with snow and sets a few big rocks on the tin top. The blood will leak into the earth and opossums will be by to clean up the brains. Spring couldn't come a day sooner.

Anna sits in her car outside the funeral home, her hands gripping the steering wheel. The heater blasts the faint odor of exhaust over her. She turns the car off. Large snowflakes drop and melt on the windshield. It's so cold it doesn't take long for them to start to stick. The car is covered with snow before she finally gets out and goes inside. One of the funeral home greeters opens the door for her, and she murmurs a thanks. When he offers to take her coat, she shakes her head and turns toward the sanctuary.

Goddamn, all funeral homes smell like dying flowers and old woman funk, sweet and moldy. Anna feels dizzy. A cold sweat breaks out on her back. She wishes she had left her coat at the door. She sees Rhonda's mother sitting in a large overstuffed chair at the front, her eyes blank, and she barely raises her head when people speak to her. Too many Zannies, Anna thinks. Through a break in the crowd, Anna sees the edges of the silver caskets set end to end and a flash of light pink. Someone touches her elbow and she jumps.

"Damn it, Flynn," she says under her breath.

"You are as pale as the moon," Flynn answers.

"I don't feel too good."

They shuffle forward in line, and Anna averts her eyes so she doesn't have to look at anyone who may be looking at her. They bypass Rhonda's mother. She's hopeless. Another of the funeral home helpers ushers them forward to the first silver casket lined with light pink. There are all sorts of things in the casket with Rhonda – a homemade blanket, flowers, a rattle, a baby doll – and Anna sees where the mortician filled in the bullet wound with putty that doesn't quite match Rhonda's skin tone, and Anna's eye flicker back to the baby doll.

"Fucking hell," Anna whispers. It's not a baby doll. It's Rhonda's baby, a baby girl, and she's tiny and beautiful and perfect, and she's dead. Anna can't stop looking at her. She's so *pretty*. Her head is round and has a wisp of blonde hair. Her cheeks aren't full, but they aren't hollow either. She has ten little fingers, and Anna wants to feel the unnatural strength of then clutching her own. She doesn't realize she is reaching forward until Flynn touches her arm and says her name. It is then she remembers, Rhonda was eight months pregnant. Anna looks at Flynn.

"She could have lived. Maybe. . . maybe if I'd gone inside. . . maybe."

Flynn pushes her away from the casket, wraps her

hand around the back of Anna's neck, and leans in.

"No, Anna. It was instant. You hear me? There was nothing you could do."

"Yes there was. I had the money."

Flynn turns Anna away from the crowd and propels her through the funeral home with a hand on her lower back.

"I had the money, Flynn. If I'd just given. . ."

"Shut up," Flynn hisses.

The greeter doesn't have time to open the door before they barrel through it. Flynn grabs Anna's hand and leads her around the building out of the wind. Anna sucks in the cold air like she's drowning.

"What are you talking about?"

Anna puts her hands in her hair and squeezes her head. A burning starts at the top of her nose and spreads to her eyes. She tells Flynn about the doctor, the pills, and the dealing.

"I got the extra pills, but it wasn't enough. I had the money and I hid it. I knew if I gave it to them I'd never see it again, and I'd spend that much more time building it up again. But, I didn't think Bill would have them killed."

"Bill?" Flynn asks. There is a subtle shift of energy as Anna realizes what she's said.

"Bill?" Flynn repeats, and Anna nods.

"He was there the day before. They owed him money."

Flynn looks into the sky. Snowflakes rush toward her, and as they enter the refracted light from the funeral home, they sparkle, like hundreds of fluffy diamonds.

"So you lied," Flynn says, "Were you lying when you said you didn't know who it was?"

Flynn's words slice through her.

"No! It was too dark, but I know it wasn't Bill. I didn't see that white hair."

"Of course not! He had one of his lackeys do it! Our kin! Did that dawn on you?"

"Goddamn it, Flynn! Back off! I don't know! Maybe he had somebody else do it!"

Flynn shakes her head, "You need to tell Manny."

163

Anna steps back.

"Manny? Since when do you call him Manny?" And Anna remembers him watching Flynn that night, the energy, the knowing, "Are you seeing him?"

"I am," Flynn says. There is no hesitation, only a cocksure, defiant Flynn.

The burning starts between Anna's eyes again, and she clenches her fists.

"You'd sell your family out for a piece of ass?"

"Oh, that's rich, Anna, considering what you've been selling, and unless my memory fails me, there's a dead baby in there. Who sold her out?"

"You are a goddamn judgmental cunt!"

Flynn steps closer, puts her finger into Anna's chest, and looks her in the eye.

"When one half of my family stops killing babies, and the other half stops lying about it, I'll stop being a cunt, until then, fuck you," Flynn says, and walks away into the blowing snow.

Bill drives Danny to a hotel in Beckley. He wants to take him to his sister's house in North Carolina, but he doesn't have time. Bill has to be seen, be visible.

"I'm really sorry, Daddy."

"It's all right, son, just, if the police come, don't talk to 'em. You call me, okay?"

Danny doesn't answer, and Bill goes up to the room with him.

"It's gonna be all right, buddy, okay? You just lay low here for a few weeks and let this shit blow over, and I'll call ya, I'll call ya every day."

But Bill isn't the only one calling Danny. Danny's girlfriend, Bunny, is also calling him, and Bunny went to the funeral home. Seeing the baby in the casket freaks her out, and she calls Danny crying. Danny sits on the bed among empty pizza boxes rubbing his forehead. He tells her to stop, but Bunny doesn't hear him and keeps talking until Danny yells at her.

"Shut the fuck up, Bunny!" Bunny hangs up on him.

He hasn't slept well and his head feels heavy. He knows he will go to jail for what Ricky did, as sure as he had pulled the trigger himself. If he tells what happened, his dad may kill him. He heard what Bill said to Mike. Danny watched from a window as Ricky and Mike got into Mike's truck, and he was still standing there when Mike came back alone. When Bill told him to pack some clothes, Danny had done so with the understanding that he wasn't coming back alive, and he wished he had said good-bye to his sister, Jessie, more so than anyone else, even Bunny.

He didn't think he could bear to speak to Jessie. She'd be so damn disappointed in him, he just, he couldn't bear it. So, when he does make the call to say good-bye, he does it when he is most sure she isn't going to be home, and the relief that spreads through him when the answering machine picks up is the most peace he's had since he and Ricky knocked on that trailer door.

"Hey, Sissy J., I just wanted to tell ya that I love ya. Bye."

It is Bill and the hotel manager who find him two days later, and in that moment Bill is broken beyond healing.

The incessant ringing of the telephone wakes Deputy Joe Thornhill. The ringing stops, there is a pause as the answering machine clicks, he hears the greeting, muffled by walls and distance, a distinct beep, a click, and within moments the phone starts ringing again. Damn. Where the hell is Jessie, and who is so hell-bent on raising them?

Before Joe can pull his pants on, the answering machine clicks again. He can smell coffee and bacon. The phone starts ringing again. He jerks the bedroom door open.

"Jessie?" There is a stillness, a heaviness, in the air. Joe grabs his gunbelt and pulls his service revolver before going down the hallway. The answering machine clicks again, and before the message can begin, the caller hangs up. Joe peeks around the corner of the dining room. Jessie sits at the table, her head in her hands. The phone begins to ring again, but she doesn't move.

"*Jessie?*"

She looks up at him and in her eyes is the same glassy miscomprehension he had seen sixteen years earlier when her husband, Cleve, had been killed in the mines leaving her a widow with three small children.

Joe has not always been a police officer. Once, he too rolled on the mantrip miles deep inside a mountain to mine the black gold. He knew Cleve his whole life up to that point. He knew Jessie too, and most of her three or five or seven siblings, depending on who you asked and how gracious her father, Moonshine Bill, was being at the time. Not that he is known for his graciousness. He is better known for his moonshining, drug dealing, womanizing, and almost magic ability to slips through the fingers of the law like a greased pig. Joe always suspected bribes, but never could prove it.

After fourteen years and the last of Bill's illegitimate children, his wife, Lydia, had had enough and divorced him and moved away to parts unknown, just like that. She left all of her children behind. It was no surprise when Jessie quit school, married Cleve, and had a baby before she turned seventeen. Cleve was also a Mullins. Chances were great he and Jessie were distant cousins, but Joe couldn't remember a time that Jessie wasn't tagging after Cleve, nor a time when Cleve wasn't crazy about her.

It was on those trips underground that Cleve filled his ears with stories about Jessie and the kids, and he was always willing to flash a new photograph that he kept in the top of his hard hat, his way of carrying his family with him wherever he went. Cleve was content in the mines and with his family, and often Joe wished he had that same contentment with his wife. He loved his two kids, but he and Sally had only been dating for three months when she became pregnant. They both struggled through their senior year before getting married.

It was eleven years before they admitted it never should have happened. Sally was livid when he left the mines, and Joe never felt close enough to her to explain why. The pay cut from miner to police officer, the loss of the two week trip to Myrtle Beach with other mining families, the loss of the status, it just pissed her off, and there wasn't enough love to facilitate forgiveness.

Joe never told Sally how the belt snapped and trapped Cleve between the continuous miner and the rock face. He never told her how he reached out to Cleve and took his hand as Cleve whispered Jessie's name before dying. The memory haunted Joe for years, and even more so, the wish he had taken his glove off, and Cleve's glove, so the man felt human flesh in his last moments.

Joe shuffled through the mourning line, but at the last moment he turned and walked away, unable to look into Jessie's empty eyes. But, the Lord does not let cowards rest, and at four-thirty Joe went back to Mahone Chapel where Jessie and the family were sitting up with Cleve through the night, a last concession to Cleve's mother, Clara.

Cleve and Jessie's eldest child, Flynn, lay on one of the pews, her fingers brushing the pitted wood floor, drool soaking into the rough maroon cushion. The elder Mullinses sat with their chins drooped onto their chests, their white hair like halos.

Jessie sat in the front pew with Clara, Cleve's two sisters, one of her own, and several of her aunts. She was the only one awake, and she turned her head as he came down the aisle. She stood and met him at the very spot she and Cleve had taken their vows, before his casket, and took his hands in hers.

"They told me you was with him. Must have been hard for ya. I appreciate it. 'Preciate you bein' here."

Her voice was soft and calm, rehearsed, as though she had committed certain gratitude to memory. She rubbed his arms as he broke down, and not wanting to be a coward, he choked out, "His last word was your name," because a woman ought to know when she is loved and cherished.

Jessie bowed her head and grabbed the top of the pew before sliding onto the floor. Joe knelt beside her, and they clung to one another like conspirators until their eyes were raw, their noses ran, and their heads pounded. Later that morning, with her youngest, Booker, slung on her hip, she lifted her miscomprehending eyes to his as he stood at the end of the last pew.

The phone rings again and Joe jerks the receiver off the hook.

"Hello!"

There is a pause.

"Joe? Joe, where's Mom?"

Jessie shakes her head, pushes away from the table, and goes into the hallway.

"I want you to tell me what's going on, Flynn."

Joe goes after her, pushing open the same screen door that slammed just minutes before, steps onto the porch, and through the silent arched trellis where in summertime kaleidoscopic rainbows of blooms nod in the breeze, sunflowers stand like sentries along the sidewalk, and the endless buzzing of bees and hummingbirds, whirring cicada and grasshopper wings, cawing crows, yakking blue jays, and murmurations of starlings were heard, but not today. Today the sky hangs low, the wind has bite and spits snow into the silence.

Jessie stands with one hand on a Langsroth hive where inside the bees huddle and vibrate to warm themselves and their queen. Perhaps, in her own way, Jessie can feel that warmth. How many times had he watched her thin shoulders during football games or planting flowers or leaning over the hives? How many times had he touched her there, that space between her shoulder blades? He had dreamed of it more times than he had done it, he knew that. So often he had watched from a distance – slim, restless Flynn reading a book while around her parents and grandparents cheered, Booker

168

bouncing and hyper cheering for his older brother, Gary, and often among them, little Danny, Jessie's youngest brother. He was willowy and, unlike the rest of them, a towhead. He had been three when Lydia left, and maybe more than once he had been referred to as "an accident."

Until he got old enough to do Bill's bidding, Danny was an afterthought to everyone but Jessie. He was more like a son than a brother, more like a brother than an uncle. Until a few years ago, he had his own room at Jessie's, that is, until the gangly coltish young man finally caught the eye of the father he longed to please. He quit his classes at the community college and tagged after Bill "like a damned dog," Jessie said, the tiny muscle in her jaw flexing.

Now, her brother, her son, the one who called her Sissy J. is gone, and worse, at his own hand. It will only get harder. Joe goes to her, and again, they kneel.

Anna has a small change of heart when it isn't Manny who comes to the gas station, but two other State Troopers she doesn't know. They have no problem pulling her away from the cash register and questioning her again, pushing for more information. There are no heavy black lines. They did not see Rhonda with her hands on her belly, they did not see a beautiful dead baby in a pink casket. Their hearts are not falling or breaking or hurting. They know what they want and she gives to them. So it surprises her when the Trooper asks about her cousin, Danny.

"Danny? Why? He wouldn't do something like this."

"When was the last time you saw him?"

"I don't know. Christmas, maybe? Why? I mean, seriously, Danny didn't do this."

"Did you see Danny the night of the murders?"

"No! I didn't see who it was."

"When did you last see Ricky Belcher?"

A chill passes through her as though someone walked on her grave. Her fingertips go numb, and then her lips, and her vision shifts. She sees the gun.

169

Pop!

The cry of a newborn erupts from thin air and dissipates.

The gun moves.

Pop!

Anna follows the hand to the arm to the shoulder to the face of Ricky Belcher.

"Ma'am?" Anna blinks.

"I don't have anything to do with Ricky Belcher, and I wish I could tell you I saw him that night, but I didn't."

When she goes back inside, her boss tells her he thinks it's best if she goes home for the rest of the day. The dismissal flies all over her then sticks in her craw.

"Oh, fuck that," Anna says, "I quit. I'm sick of this shit."

"Well, you don't have to be that way about it!"

"Yeah, yeah I do!"

When Anna gets to the intersection, she doesn't turn toward home, she turns toward Flynn's. She stews the entire way, and it pisses her off even more when Flynn isn't home until she spots Flynn's car at Jessie's, still a momma's girl after all these years. She couldn't even move further away than the crack of Jessie's ass.

First, it was poor Flynn, who lost her daddy, and then it was the mighty Flynn, the over-achiever who quit school at sixteen, not because she was pregnant or failing or lazy, but because she was bored. The mighty Flynn who went to college, not the community college like all the other poor saps, but a university, and then to another university for her law degree – the first person in their family to graduate from college.

Whoop-dee-do, and where has it gotten her? She's still living in the same dingy community with coal trucks throwing up dust, coal miners with their broken backs and black lungs, punks in jacked-up trucks with Confederate flags and no futures, slurry ponds, rust water, teenagers spitting out babies, and desperate addicts leaning over a doctor's table.

Fuck that. Fuck it all.

Flynn watches Anna slam the door of her car and stalk toward the door. Something has her back up, and Flynn figures she knows what it is. Instead of going to the door, Flynn sits at the kitchen table and lets Joe take care of it.

Anna isn't surprised when Joe answers the door, but she is surprised that the house is so quiet. It's abnormal.

"Hey, Joe. How's it goin'?"

"Been better. I suppose you're here to see Jessie and Flynn. They're in the kitchen. I know they'll appreciate you stopping by."

The fight is starting to ebb in Anna, and his words almost stamp it out completely.

"What? What do you mean?"

"I figured you's here to pay your respects."

It isn't Joe's way to play games, he's normally a direct person, but he is a little pissed at Anna, but even more protective of Jessie and her kids.

"I. . . what happened?"

"Danny," Joe says, "He killed himself. Bill found him this morning."

The news shakes Anna to her core. No wonder the cops asked about him. Jesus Christ. She wants to ask if he left a note, but she figures he did, otherwise they wouldn't have asked about Ricky. She knows it wasn't Danny who pulled the trigger, but now she does know he was the second person there. The burning starts between her eyes again.

"I'm surprised no one's told ya. Phone's been ringing off the hook."

"I was at work," she murmurs, ashamed now of her anger and jealousy. What a deep green vein it is.

Angeline stands on the leeward side of the funeral home with Virgie and Vicki. The sun is out, the snow has melted, but the wind is still wicked cold. As Angeline exhales, it grabs the smoke from her mouth and bears it away with a trail of frosty breath following. Some of her cousins are drinking Budweiser from a cooler stashed in the trunk of an old Buick.

"Can you believe that shit?" Virgie asks.

"I've learned to believe just about anything out of this family," Angeline says.

It has been a wild ride in the year since she came back. She stayed with Jessie, mostly, in Danny's old room. Flynn helped her get a divorce, taught her to drive, and helped her get an old beat-up car after she finally sold the trailer and the little bit of property. She also started classes at the community college. It is a slow process, and every once in a while Flynn asks if she is seeing the counselor she recommended. Angeline tells her no, but she is thinking about it again. She had been seeing a guy from school, but after a while, he reminded her of Dale. . . and Jack. She realizes the problem is with her, something deep inside that refuses to release her until she digs it out.

"How much longer?" Vicki asks. She is hung over and considering a little hair of the dog to take the edge off.

"Five minutes later than the last time you asked me," Virgie says. Vicki rolls her eyes and makes a face at her sister. A car pulls into the parking lot and someone closes the trunk of the Buick and the beers are sat inside on the floorboards and the door shut. Then they see why when Jessie, Flynn, Joe, and Manny get out. They stop and speak, there are hugs and handshakes.

Vicki notices another car. It pulls into the lower driveway and darts into a distant space. She watches it for another minute or two, but no one gets out. Probably someone getting high or waiting on drugs. It happens all over. Speaking of, maybe one of her kin has a Zannie they can part with, hell, for that matter, she'll ask Anna. Huh. Really piss her off.

"Where's Anna?"

"If she were up your ass, you'd know," Virgie says.

"Well you don't have to be such a bitch about it!

Goddamn!"

"You're askin' more questions than a two year old. I'm surprised you haven't asked to go to the bathroom yet."

Virgie doesn't handle death well, and she's handling this even worse. She has gnawed all of her fingernails down to the quick, and whereas she normally finds humor in every situation, her cousin laying inside his silver casket has taken the spirit right out of her.

"I can't believe they've kept their love affair secret for so long," Vicki says, gesturing to Flynn and Manny, "Must have pissed you off, Angie, her snitching your man like that."

Angie lets out an exaggerated sigh, "Good God Almighty, he was never my man! Do you always have to be such a cunt, Vicki?"

"Here now," Virgie says, holding up her hand, "They ain't no need for name callin'."

"I'm gonna call it like I see it, and I'd swear you're jealous, Vicki."

Vicki snorts, "I ain't jealous over no sand nigger."

Suddenly, Vicki flies into the side of the funeral home. Sugar Ray had come up behind her and shoved her. There's a trickle of blood from a cut under Vicki's eye.

"How many times have I talked to you about using that word, Victoria? And not only are you a bigot, but you're also a goddamn liar, because that sure wasn't what it looked like when Robert kicked your drunk ass out on Shavers Ridge, and Trooper Manny brought you to my house. You were on him like stink on shit. He had to peel you off of him like a fruit roll-up. I'm surprised you didn't start humping his leg. Goddamn embarrassin'. This whole family has lost it goddamn mind! Quit drinkin' in the parking lot!" She screams. The cousins turn and look at her, some have enough grace to look embarrassed, but most have enough gall to raise a can in her direction.

"You're a . . ." Vicki starts.

"Oh, shut up! Just shut up!" Sugar Ray says, "Before I black your other eye. Service starts in thirty minutes. I hope to

God we can make it that far. Jesus take the wheel."

Sugar Ray stomps around to the private entrance and slams the door.

"She seems a little stressed," Virgie says, "and get that nasty look off your face. You deserved that and more. I've warned you, don't be sayin' the N-word, and definitely don't be sayin' it in front of your sister. Her husband is your brother-in-law, her kids are your niece and nephew, I don't care what color they are."

Vicki dabs at the cut with the sleeve of her shirt and doesn't say anything, for once.

Anna is late getting to the funeral home, but before she can shimmy past two other latecomers into the last row, which had been set up with folding chairs for extra room, she hears,

"Psst, Anna!" Instead she has no choice but to make the walk of shame to the third row and squeeze in beside of Vicki.

"Didn't know if you'd make it," Virgie whispers, leaning over Vicki, "wouldn't blame you if you didn't."

Vicki shoves back on her.

"Get off me."

"What happened to your face?" Anna asks.

"Sugar bodychecked her into the side of the building."

"Sshhhh."

The service is short and devoid of the usual entreaties to straighten your life up and come to God. There was no awkward silence or rustling when no one came forward. Instead, Big Mike and Grim flank Bill as he steps to the casket one last time. Bill reaches out and touches his son's face. When he turns, his head hangs. Anna has never seen him that way, of course, he has never lost a child either, but still, something about him is different.

Jessie touches Danny also. Then she pats his crossed hands before turning and walking down the aisle with Joe, Flynn and Manny on their heels.

"Hey," Vicki elbows her, "You got any Zannies?"

"Why? You want some?"

"Yeah, you know, a few, three or four."

"Twenty bucks."

That was why Anna was late. She was waiting for her pills at the pharmacy, just one last time. Vicki makes a face.

"You're gonna charge me?"

"Life ain't free, sister," Anna says, deferring a trip to the casket to fall in behind Flynn. The rest of the row follows her.

Jessie reaches the last row and stops, digging her toes in like a mule.

It's always the last row, she thinks. It had happened when she was six months old, or so her mother said, when she saw Jessie's sister, Rose, for the first time. And it had happened again when Cleve died, but that time it was Joe in that back pew, and she *knew*, what, she would never be able to tell you. That's how the knowing is – no explanations, just a sight, a feeling.

And today, a ghost stands in the back row, and Jessie stares at her, unable to move and unable to speak.

People are starting to pile up behind them, and Flynn touches Jessie's arm. It is rigid, and Flynn believes she can feel the heat of Jessie's skin through her suit.

"Mom?" It is then she looks at the woman in the last row. Flynn doesn't recognize her at first, not until she notices her startling eyes – so blue they're silver. Like mine, Flynn thinks.

"What's going on? Who's that woman?" Vicki asks.

"Oh my God," Virgie says, "I think, I think it's Lydia."

"Lydia?" Vicki and Anna say together, and they both crane their necks for a better look.

"Who's Lydia?" Angeline asks above the murmuring, and she too cranes her neck, but it isn't the woman at the end

175

of the row that draws her attention, but the skinny, bleached blonde beside of her, her arms crossed over her chest.

"Jessie's mom, walked out on 'em when Danny was just a little thing. Oh my God," Virgie says again, "Is that?"

"My mom," says Angeline. Her voice is hard and her face flushes with anger and hurt. Angeline pushes through the throng, elbows Manny to the side, and is stopped by Flynn's arm.

"Angie, don't."

"Get of my way, Flynn." Angeline *wants* her mother to see her. And she does. Josie raises her hand to her face and then reaches out to Angeline.

"Angeline, baby."

And Josie's face swims and distorts as Angeline slides the folding chairs out of the way. They skitter like rattles on a diamondback. She punches Josie, a quick, neat jab that snaps Josie's head back. There is a collective gasp as she staggers backward, sending her own chair into the wall.

"You cunt! You left me!"

Lydia helps Josie stand. Her lip is split and blood drips onto her dress.

"He would've killed me if I took you!"

"Damn you for leaving me," Angeline's voice shakes, breaks, hissing, deeper than anger, a black twisted rage coiled inside of her, "with him."

Angeline turns and pushes her way out toward the door. Jessie looks at Lydia.

"You're too late," Jessie says, and walks away.

Anna sits with Angeline in her room at Jessie's house. Angeline tears a wad of tissues into tiny pieces, her hands still shaking. Anna dips into her purse, pulls out a pill bottle, shakes a pill out, and breaks it in half.

"Here, just to calm you down."

Vicki huffs behind her and Anna hands her the other half.

"You said I could have four."

"Goddamn it, Vicki."

Anna shakes the bottle again, and when Vicki holds out her hand, Anna says,

"I said you can have them for twenty bucks. I'll give you the half for free."

Vicki digs into her purse and pulls out a ten and two fives and takes the pills from Anna.

"This is the first time I've ever really liked you," she quips on her way out of the bedroom.

"Well that's one more time than I've ever liked you," Anna says.

Vicki, stops, turns, and sticks her tongue out.

"You really meant that, didn't ya?" Angeline asks.

"Yeah," Anna says, "but anyway, look, I'm leaving. I got some money saved up, I guess you know from where, but I can't stay here anymore. I thought maybe you might want to go with me, I mean, after you get out of school, you could come up. You can go to school in Charleston, I'm going, I think. Just, you know, think about it."

Angeline nods her head.

"Actually, that sounds pretty damn good," her hands are steadier, "Yeah, we could do that. Be easier with two of us working, and you know, I could help you with Noah."

"What? What's that look on your face?"

"I'm afraid," Angeline admits, "I'm afraid if I leave I'll never come back, but I'm afraid if I don't leave, I never will."

Anna takes the money from behind the light fixture and with it, still rolled up, is the money she found on the ground in front of Rhonda's door, twenty-nine hundred dollars. She rents an apartment and a small moving truck from Charleston and leaves her car in their lot. She moves all of her own stuff, not that it's much, straps Noah in the front seat, and waits while Ernie does a walk through. There's still police tape across Rhonda's front porch. Ernie comes out.

"Well, ya know, I don't remember the carpet being

stained under the window."

"Ernie, I want my deposit back. Stop fucking around."

It isn't above Ernie to wonder if maybe Anna didn't set Rhonda and Dave up. She probably has a little more of Moonshine Bill in her than she cares to admit. Walk softly, talk softly, and carry your family name. Ernie gives her the money.

Acknowledgements

Thank you to my husband, Gary, and my son, Nate, both of whom took the time to listen to the very first incarnations of these stories and were wise enough to tell me when to dial it back.

And again to my husband Gary for remaining unfailingly supportive of my dream.

And again to my son Nate who suffered through take-out food and separation while I finished my Master's degree.

Thank you to my fellow Goddardites, advisors, and support staff, who also heard some of the first incarnations of these stories for your support and encouragement.

Thank you to Shelly Weathers, my sister of Southern Gothic, for your treasured feedback.

Thank you to Erica Hays for my kickass book cover.

Thank you to my family for an endless supply of stories to dig into.

Blessed Be to my cousins, Nicole Kessler and Kama King. Our stories have yet to be told.

Thank you to all of my friends like family that are too numerous to list who have supported me over the years, especially my Bistro family and my blog family.

I love you all.